How to use this book

This book is designed to be read initially by children and adults together. It is not an explanation of what cancer is, but a book about the impact the diagnosis of childhood cancer can have on a sibling's life. It is a starting point for discussion, giving the adult a way in to ask about the child's own experience of difficult situations. On each page one of the illustrations has been left for the child to colour in.

First Edition

Text © Cancer Link Aberdeen & North 2005
Illustrations © Cancer Link Aberdeen & North 2005

International Standard Book No. 0-9551642-0-6

978-0-9551642-0-0

Published by:

Cancer Link Aberdeen & North
CLAN House
Caroline Place
Aberdeen
AB25 2TH

Printed by Halcon Print and Design, Stonehaven.

MIKKI HAS CANCER

By Eileen Wheeler

&

Illustrated by Iiris Maanoja

Mikki is my little brother. He has blonde hair that sticks up like a hedgehog and green eyes that are a bit like the cat's. He has just had his 6th birthday party and he has cancer.

When I first heard Mikki had cancer I didn't believe it. I thought cancer was something old people got, not children, and not my brother.

The doctor at the hospital told mum and dad about the cancer, and then they told my granny and grandad, nana and I'm not sure who else. I was scared because I hadn't seen adults crying before. So it had to be really serious. They tried to hide their tears from me but I would catch them sometimes.

Mikki had mum to himself all the time in hospital, and he got loads of presents even though it wasn't Christmas or his birthday. Everyone brought presents to the ward or sent parcels to our house for Mikki. He didn't even say thank you for them! Nobody sent me a present and I was trying to be brave and good.

Just after we found
out about the cancer,
mum and Mikki went to the hospital to stay there, so he could start
his treatment. I didn't want Mikki to be alone, but I wanted my mum
at home too. It was lonely without Mikki in the house and a bit scary.
And what if mum was too busy caring for Mikki and forgot about me?

I didn't like it when Mikki
had to stay in hospital to
get his chemotherapy medicine, or
was rushed in to hospital when I was at school.
It was lonely at home, especially at night. I used to climb into his bed
and fall asleep there. I missed Mikki and didn't want him to be ill. I
wanted it to be like before.

Sometimes I didn't know who would collect me from school and I'd be bad-tempered all day. Mum tried to be there, but when Mikki was poorly it was nana or Sam's mum or Liam's mum or Matthew's mum who collected me.

At school the other
children always asked lots of questions or
said stupid things. 'Where's Mikki?' 'Why does
Mikki have a bald head?' 'Is he going to die?' 'Are you going
to get cancer too?' 'You can't play with us, we don't want to catch
cancer'. I know you can't catch cancer, but I wished they would leave
me alone. My teacher, Mrs Ross, was kind to me and each morning
asked me quietly if I was okay. I know I can tell her if I am upset.

When Mikki was at home mum fussed over him. If he said he was hot or had a sore tummy she always listened to him and stopped everything to check his temperature straight away. Sometimes I wanted to shout 'What about me? I'm here too!' Sometimes I pretended I had a sore leg or sore tummy to get mum to check me out too.

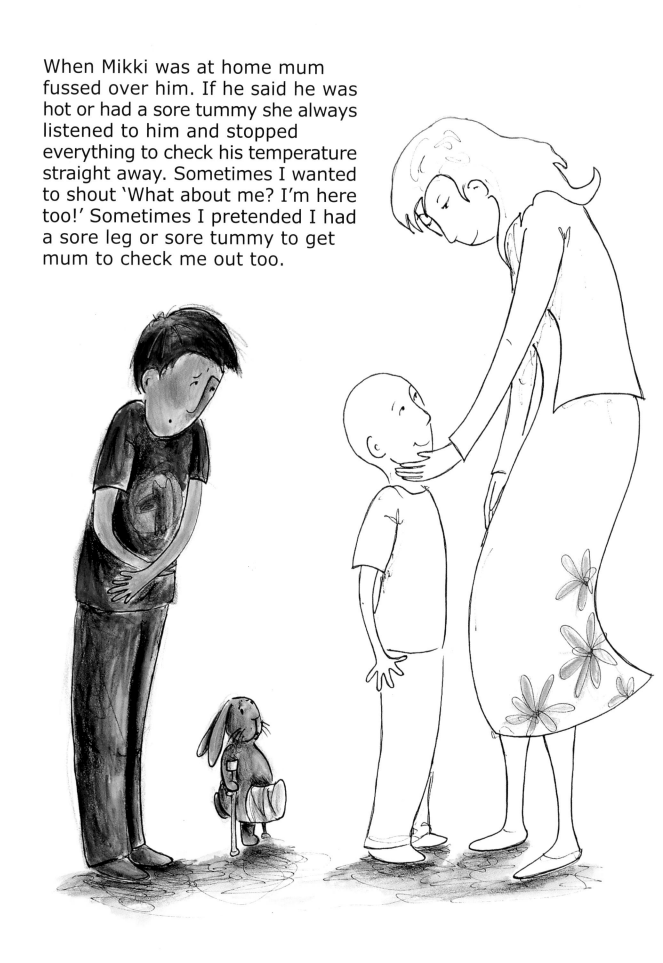

If Mikki didn't eat his dinner mum said it was okay, but I had to eat mine or got into trouble. When Mikki was taking some of his medicine he was horrible to mum and he didn't get into trouble for giving her cheek. I always do. That's not fair. Mum says it's the medicine being horrid, not Mikki, but I'm not sure.

I like it when I can play in the garden with Mikki, at chasing or pretend fighting. It is like it was before he was ill, but then Mikki will say 'Don't hit me, I've got cancer. I'll tell mum on you.' That makes me angry because he still hits me as hard as he can.

I am looking forward to Mikki just being Mikki again, without his wiggly, his feeding tube, with hair that stays in and not having to go to the hospital all the time, that won't happen for a while but I hope it will not be too long. Then we can have proper pretend fights and chases, I will teach him to swim and we can do other things we are missing out on at the moment.

Eileen Wheeler is the support worker for children and young people with CLAN, a cancer support charity. Her role is to support any child or young person affected by cancer, whether as a patient, relative or friend. She can provide information at a level suited to the individual, and allow the child to explore his/her feelings in a safe and secure environment. Support can be offered on an individual basis or in groups. Eileen is a qualified social worker, who previously worked at the Royal Aberdeen Children's Hospital where she supported families who had a child diagnosed with cancer.

CLAN is a registered charity which has been operating in North East Scotland, Orkney and Shetland since 1983. It provides support and information to anyone affected by cancer.

For Oliver Edward, Fiona and Nick's much-loved little boy

ACKNOWLEDGEMENTS

Fiona wishes to thank all of her recipe testers, especially Caroline Butler for her conscientious feedback notes, and Nick, Sophie and Iona for their support during her pregnancy. She would also like to thank Trevor Wing and his staff at The Women's Natural Health Practice, especially Elke, Olga and Naomi, for all their help before and during her pregnancy. They could not come more highly recommended.

Patrick and Susannah wish to thank the many couples they have had the privilege to work with – and all the healthy babies who've arrived in this world as a result of their parents' desire to embrace the optimum nutrition approach to fertility and pregnancy.

Finally, Patrick, Fiona and Susannah wish to thank their editors Gill, Rebecca and especially Jillian for their hard work in producing this very special book.

Disclaimer

While all the nutrients and dietary changes referred to in this book have been proven safe, those seeking help for specific medical conditions are advised to consult a qualified nutritional therapist, doctor or equivalent health professional. The recommendations given in this book are solely intended as education and information and should not be taken as medical advice. Neither the authors nor the publisher accept liability for readers who choose to self-prescribe.

All supplements should be kept out of reach of infants and young children.

Guide to Abbreviations and Measures

Most vitamins are measured in milligrams or micrograms. Vitamins A, D and E are also measured in International Units (IUs), a measurement designed to standardise the various forms of these vitamins, which have different potencies.

1 gram (g) = 1000 milligrams (mg) = 1,000,000 micrograms (mcg)

1mcg of retinal (1mcg RE) = 3.3 IUs of vitamin A
1mcg RE of beta-carotene = 6mcg of beta-carotene
100IUs of vitamin D = 2.5mcg
100IUs of vitamin E = 67mg

The
Perfect Pregnancy
Cookbook

BOOST FERTILITY AND PROMOTE A HEALTHY PREGNANCY
WITH OPTIMUM NUTRITION

patrick
HOLFORD

Fiona McDonald Joyce & Susannah Lawson

PIATKUS

First published in Great Britain in 2010 by Piatkus
Copyright © Patrick Holford and Fiona McDonald Joyce 2010

The moral right of the authors has been asserted

A CIP catalogue record for this book
is available from the British Library

ISBN 978-0-7499-2912-1

Printed and bound in China by C&C Offset Printing Co., Ltd
Recipe photography © Ian Greig Garlick
Home economist: Lorna Brash
Designed and illustrated by D.R. ink. www.d-r-ink.com

Piatkus
An imprint of
Little, Brown Book Group
100 Victoria Embankment
London EC4Y 0DY

An Hachette UK Company
www.hachette.co.uk
www.piatkus.co.uk

Picture credits
Nick Morris: pp 3. Ian Greig Garlick: pp 6, 62, 65, 68, 70, 73, 76, 79, 83, 85, 86, 93, 98, 100, 101, 105, 108, 113, 115, 117, 121, 126, 128, 133, 138, 141, 145, 150, 154, 157, 158, 163, 166, 168, 173, 178. Tetra Images/Corbis: pp 10. Martin Sundberg/Corbis: pp 21. Larry Williams/Corbis: pp 22. Sandra Ivany/Brand X/Corbis: pp 26. Simon Katzer/Getty: pp 30. Image Source/Corbis: pp 38. Marnie Burkhart/Corbis: pp 44. Rolf Bruderer/Corbis: pp 47. Artiga Photo/Corbis: pp 52. Corbis: pp 61

ABOUT THE AUTHORS

Patrick Holford

Patrick Holford BSc, DipION, FBANT, NTCRP is a leading spokesman on nutrition in the media. He is author of 30 health books, translated into over 20 languages and selling over a million copies worldwide, including the *Optimum Nutrition Bible* and *Optimum Nutrition for Your Child*.

In 1984 Patrick founded the Institute for Optimum Nutrition (ION), an independent educational charity, and was involved in groundbreaking research showing that multivitamins can increase children's IQ scores – research that was published in the *Lancet* and the subject of a *Horizon* documentary in the 1980s. He was one of the first promoters of the importance of zinc, antioxidants, essential fats, low-GL diets and homocysteine-lowering B vitamins such as folic acid.

He is director of the Food for the Brain Foundation and director of the Brain Bio Centre, the Foundation's treatment centre. He is an honorary fellow of the British Association of Nutritional Therapy, as well as a member of the Nutrition Therapy Council.

Fiona McDonald Joyce

Fiona McDonald Joyce, DipION, mBANT is a nutritional therapist and cookery consultant who specialises in creating healthy recipes that don't compromise on taste. With Patrick, Fiona is co-author of *The Low-GL Diet Cookbook*, *Smart Food for Smart Kids*, *The Holford 9-Day Liver Detox* and *Food GLorious Food*. She recently gave birth to Oliver, and devised most of the recipes for this book while she was pregnant.

Susannah Lawson

Susannah Lawson, DipION, mBANT, is a health journalist and a nutritional therapist. She graduated from the Institute for Optimum Nutrition with distinction and has been working with couples and individuals to help them naturally overcome fertility problems and other health issues since 2003. With Patrick, Susannah is co-author of *Optimum Nutrition Before During and After Pregnancy* and *Optimum Nutrition Made Easy*. She also writes for mainstream media, lectures and runs workshops about health and nutrition, and is currently training in the field of energetic medicine.

Contents

Introduction

We believe that creating a baby is the most miraculous act we humans can achieve. It's not surprising then that we also believe it shouldn't be left to luck or chance. As would-be parents you should take advantage of the wealth of scientific information now available – but sadly not yet in the mainstream – to ensure you give your baby the best start in life.

We know, for example, that women who eat a good diet and supplement with a multivitamin and mineral during pregnancy give birth to healthier babies. Thanks to the pioneering research of Professor David Barker, we also know that poor maternal diet can increase the risk of a baby developing diseases such as diabetes or heart disease in later life.

The valuable work of the preconceptual care charity Foresight has shown that optimising the health and diet of both parents can dramatically reduce infertility and increase the chances of a healthy pregnancy with a healthy baby at the end of it. With one in six UK couples today suffering with fertility problems, one in four pregnancies ending in miscarriage and one in 17 babies born with some sort of birth defect, this approach truly offers the best solution to ensuring the health and continuation of the next generation. And it's far more effective. IVF has an average 22 per cent success rate, with babies born suffering a higher than average instance of birth defects. Following an optimum nutrition protocol, on the other hand, achieves a 78 per cent success rate, with fewer pregnancy problems and healthier babies.

So if you are having problems conceiving, have experienced miscarriage or pregnancy problems in the past – or are taking the enlightened approach of getting yourself and your partner into the best possible shape before you bring a new baby into the world – this book will guide you.

In Parts One and Two, we explore the key issues around optimising your diet and nutrient intake – and minimising your exposure to harmful substances – for maximum fertility and a healthy pregnancy. Then in Part Three, nutritional therapist and cookery consultant Fiona McDonald Joyce translates the theory into delicious meals and snacks to make optimum nutrition eating a genuine pleasure.

We wish you – and your future children – the very best of health.

Patrick Holford and Susannah Lawson

PART ONE

Preparing for Pregnancy

CHAPTER 1
Feeding Fertility

What you eat can make a big difference to how you feel and how your body functions. If you give yourself the very best nutritious food, then you're more likely to achieve optimum health and that means optimum fertility. Animal breeders understand this – that's why ewes are put to graze on the richest grass before the tups (male sheep) are let loose, and horses are routinely given nutrient-rich feeds to get them into the best possible condition before mare meets stallion.

But what about humans? It appears we're not treating ourselves so well. As a result, one in six couples now has problems conceiving. Conventional investigations often return a diagnosis of 'unexplained infertility' and research published in the *British Medical Journal* in August 2008 found that the initial treatments offered by the NHS are actually no more effective than giving none. The next step, IVF, can be traumatic and expensive, with less than a quarter of women actually ending up with a baby as a result.

But there is a way to increase your fertility naturally – by ensuring your body (and that of your partner) is optimally nourished. Does it work? Statistics suggest a nutritional protocol can achieve a 78 per cent success rate. Being

as healthy as possible before conception also increases your chances of having a healthy pregnancy and a healthy baby, more of which is covered in the next chapter.

So how do you get yourself in top fertile form? Diet, stress levels, weight and toxin exposure all play a role, as we explain.

Four Steps to Female Fruitfulness

Unlike men, who produce a regular supply of fresh sperm after puberty, women are born with all their eggs (or ova) in place. Your ovaries contain about two million eggs at birth, but as you age, they gradually disintegrate. By puberty there are approximately 750,000 left, and by age 45 only about 10,000 are left. Your fertility is dependent on the health of these eggs and your reproductive organs, plus your body's ability to produce the right balance of hormones to 'mature' your eggs ready for ovulation with each monthly cycle. Getting the right mix of supporting nutrients is key to this, as is regulating your weight and dealing with stress. Below are four key steps to support successful ovulation.

1. Balance Your Hormones

Hormones make things happen – for example, follicle-stimulating hormone (FSH) matures an ovum, oestrogen ensures that it is released at ovulation, and progesterone keeps it healthy during and after conception. Yet the fine balance of these hormones can often be disrupted. The mineral zinc and vitamin B_6 work together to produce and regulate female sex hormones – inadequate amounts of either nutrient can create a hormonal deficiency or imbalance. They also increase your desire for sex (which is why zinc-rich oysters are renowned as an aphrodisiac) and alleviate premenstrual problems – women who suffer from premenstrual syndrome (PMS) are often zinc deficient.

Essential fats – those found in oily fish like sardines, salmon and mackerel, and also in nuts and seeds – are also important for hormone balance. They facilitate healthy hormone functioning, so a deficiency is likely to affect your menstrual cycle and therefore your fertility.

Hormonal conditions which affect the reproductive area, such as polycystic ovary syndrome (PCOS) or endometriosis, can also impact on fertility. Balancing blood sugar is a key aim for relieving PCOS, and supporting the immune system (see page 24) can help alleviate endometriosis. As the underlying causes for specific hormone-related problems are often unique to each individual, seeking expert help from a nutritional therapist can bring real benefits.

ACTION: Eat foods rich in zinc (oysters, red meat, nuts, seeds, egg yolks, rye and oats) and B_6 (cauliflower, watercress, bananas and broccoli). Also supplement a good daily multivitamin to ensure you get at least 10mg of zinc and 25mg of B_6. To boost your essential fat intake, have a portion of oily fish twice a week and eat a handful of fresh, unsalted seeds (for example pumpkin, sunflower, flaxseeds every day, or grind up and sprinkle on cereal or salads). Seeds are also rich in zinc. If you have a specific hormone-related condition, seek the help of a nutritional therapist.

2. Clean Up Your Act

When you want to get pregnant, reducing your intake of, or exposure to, harmful substances can increase your chances of conception, as well as creating a healthier environment for your baby to develop.

According to research published in the journal *Fertility and Sterility*, drinking any alcohol at all can reduce your fertility by half – and the more you drink, the less likely you are to conceive. Another study showed that women who drank less than five units of alcohol (i.e. fewer than four small glasses of wine or 2.5 pints of beer) a week were twice as likely to conceive within six months compared with those who drank more.

Unsurprisingly, smoking hampers fertility too. A study at the Institute for Reproductive Medicine in Germany found that smoking damages the quality of eggs in ovaries, reducing the number capable of producing a baby. And cannabis, considered by some to be safer, is actually equally harmful and also linked to infertility.

Sadly, you can't even seek solace with a cup of coffee. Research has shown that caffeine –

also found in tea, chocolate and cola drinks – decreases fertility. A study in the *Lancet* found that just one cup of coffee a day can halve your chances of conceiving.

Environmental toxins should also be avoided where possible. Pollution, pesticides, toxic metals such as lead or mercury, even the chemicals in hair dye and cleaning products, can all impact negatively on fertility, as well as harming a developing baby. The problem is that these toxins don't break down but rather accumulate in your body. In the next chapter, we go into more detail on the 'anti-nutrients' to avoid and how to reduce their impact, both for fertility and during pregnancy.

ACTION: Quit or seriously limit any intake of alcohol and caffeine, and avoid all forms of tobacco. If you need help to give up any addictive substance, refer to Patrick's book *How to Quit Without Feeling S**t* (Piatkus). Limit exposure to any environmental toxins and chemicals as much as you can – for example by eating organic food (see page 20) – and ensure a good intake of antioxidant nutrients (see page 25) to help detoxify what you can't avoid. If you are concerned about past exposure, see a nutritional therapist to discuss testing for this and detoxifying your body.

3. Calm Down

Deadlines, traffic jams, difficult relationships, money worries, information overload, time pressures… Modern life is full of stress triggers.

But stress puts your body into a state of alert which hinders the smooth functioning of systems such as digestion and reproduction. Stress also burns up stores of nutrients –

especially B vitamins – which are crucial for a multitude of functions including fertility.

We know that being relaxed boosts fertility – this explains why holidays are a common time to conceive. But for most of us, taking time off is limited to a few weeks a year. The rest of the time, if you find it hard to relax, get irritable, are unable to 'shut off' from the events of the day or have trouble sleeping, stress is having a negative effect on your health – and this could impact on your fertility.

Stress experts will often say it's not the stress but the reaction that causes the problem. Unless your house burns down or someone dies, most stresses are not disasters. Thinking they are, however, can easily overwhelm you.

ACTION: Make some time every day to relax – read a book, have a warm bath or just lie down quietly for 10 minutes. If you often feel overwhelmed by stress there are many options that can help you. Learn to meditate, take up t'ai chi or yoga, have a regular massage, learn positive thinking – whatever will help you to relax and get on top of stress. The diet and supplement plan we recommended will also provide all the nutrients you need to help your body cope better with stress.

4. Optimise Your Weight

Women who are either under or over weight can experience fertility problems. Being fat phobic can also impact on hormonal health, so those who avoid eating any fat (especially the good variety) are also at risk.

Swedish research has revealed that the 'average' woman (i.e. 5ft 4in of medium build) will stop having periods at 52kg (8st 3lb). And even those who have periods but who have low body weight can be infertile.

Likewise, if you are overweight your fertility can be reduced. Even moderate obesity – classified as a body mass index of 25–30 (see below) – can reduce your chances of conception and increase the risk of miscarriage.

ACTION: For maximum fertility, you need to eat enough of the right kind of fats (see page 34) and be neither under nor over weight. As each of us has individual bone structures and body shapes, there is no definitive answer to what your normal weight should be, but the body mass index (BMI) is a useful guide. To calculate your BMI, divide your weight in kilograms (kg) by the square of your height in metres. For example, if you weigh 62kg (9st 7lb) and are 1.70m (5ft 7in) tall, your BMI is $62 \div (1.70 \times 1.70) = 21.5$. Below 20 is considered underweight, 20–25 normal and 25–30 overweight. If you want to lose weight before conception, refer to Patrick's *Low-GL Diet Bible* (Piatkus) for an effective strategy. And follow the guidelines for low-GL eating (see page 34 and the recipes in Part Three).

Turbo Charge His Sperm

Testicles don't just dangle for decoration – they are busy manufacturing fresh sperm throughout a man's adult life. It takes about four months for each batch to develop, so optimising nutrient intake and minimising toxin exposure can have a real impact on sperm quality and quantity.

As statistics show that sperm quality is diminishing – over the past 50 years, by around 50 per cent – and that men are thought to be equally responsible for infertility and up to 60 per cent of genetic abnormalities, a preconception MOT for your man can maximise your chances of conceiving quickly and having a healthy baby. Here's his three-step guide to making super sperm:

1. Cut Out Social Poisons

Most people know that smoking is bad news for health. When it comes to sperm, research has found that even a few cigarettes can reduce concentration by around a quarter. The mutagenic compounds of tobacco (and also cannabis) also damage sperm. As it takes about four months to produce sperm (a month or so more than the time taken to mature an egg) encouraging your partner to stop smoking long before you plan to try for a baby is therefore advisable.

Alcohol is also toxic to male reproductive organs and can cause significant deterioration in sperm quality – in heavy drinkers it can even result in complete infertility. Heavy and sustained smoking and drinking also depletes the body of key nutrients, especially B vitamins that are vital to reproductive health. And as for women, coffee is also bad news for men wanting to conceive. Studies have shown the higher the coffee consumption, the lower the sperm quality.

ACTION: Quit cigarettes, coffee and alcohol, ideally four months before trying to conceive. If your partner needs help quitting, Patrick's book *How to Quit Without Feeling S**t* (Piatkus) can offer support and advice.

2. Limit Exposure to Environmental Toxins

Exposure to environmental chemicals that have 'oestrogenic' effects – that is they mimic the female hormone oestrogen – is associated with declining sperm count, as well as testicular and prostate cancers. Sadly, we encounter these chemicals every day – they are found in plastics, food packaging, pesticides, paint and cosmetics.

Exposure to chemicals in the workplace – especially in agricultural, dry cleaning, manufacturing, building and paint spraying businesses – can also impact male fertility and is associated with an increase in miscarriage, still birth and birth defects in offspring.

ACTION: Opt for products that use natural ingredients, avoid having food or drink that's been heated in plastic, filter your drinking water and aim to eat organic food where possible (see page 20). If your partner's work brings him into contact with chemicals, encourage him to wear protective clothing and take regular breaks. Improved nutrition, especially a good intake of antioxidants (see page 27) can also provide enhanced protection.

3. Boost the Fertility Nutrients

Eating the diet outlined in this book will increase intake of all the essential nutrients for both of you. Particular focus should also be paid to the following:

- Zinc – of all the nutrients known to affect male fertility, zinc is perhaps the best researched. Signs of zinc deficiency include late sexual maturation, small sex organs and infertility. A lack of zinc can also damage the testes. As the average person only gets just over half the daily recommended amount of 15mg – and between 1–3mg of zinc is lost with each ejaculation – zinc deficiency in men is very common. As with women, zinc works with B_6. Boosting levels of both these nutrients can increase male fertility (see Chapter 5 for sources).

- Vitamins C and E – vitamin C has been shown to increase sperm count and motility (its ability to swim) as well as to safeguard it from damage. Studies have found that vitamin E also increases fertility.

- Essential fats – these aid hormone balance and increase substances called prostaglandins, which are often deficient in men with poor sperm quality, abnormal sperm, poor motility or low count.

- Chromium – a deficiency of this essential mineral can hinder the body's ability to make new cells, including sperm. Studies show that rodents fed on diets low in chromium have a significantly lower sperm count and decreased fertility compared to chromium-supplemented rodents.

ACTION: Encourage your partner to eat a diet rich in whole grains, fresh fruits and vegetables, oily fish, seeds, nuts and lean red meat – basically the diet and recipes outlined in this book, so he can eat the same as you. He should also supplement daily with a good-quality multivitamin and mineral containing at least 10mg of zinc, 200mg of vitamin E and 50mcg of chromium, plus an extra 1000mg of vitamin C.

Extra Help for Older Parents

The number of women having babies in their thirties and early forties has significantly increased – from 30 per cent in 1986 to 46 per cent in 2006. But fertility rates for older parents are still lower than for those in their twenties and the instance of birth defects higher. And it's not just in women where fertility declines – according to research published in the journal *Human Reproduction*, men also have a biological clock, with their chances of hitting the jackpot within six months of trying reducing by 2 per cent for every year past the age of 24. So a 40-year-old man and his partner are likely to take about a third longer to conceive than a 25 year old and his partner, regardless of the age of the women.

The main reason for this is because, for both sexes, your baby-making materials (sperm and eggs) are more prone to damage from 'oxidation', essentially the ageing process. You also have had more exposure to environmental or social toxins (pollution, pesticides, cigarette smoke, toxic metals, etc.) which can build up in the body and hinder proper hormone and nutrient function (see Chapter 2).

The good news is we have an in-built system to disarm oxidants, but this requires a plentiful supply of 'antioxidant' nutrients to work. Antioxidant nutrients include vitamins A, C and E, plus the minerals zinc and selenium. Studies have found each of these nutrients can boost fertility in both sexes. That's why the diet and supplement programme we recommend is designed to boost your intake.

There's also a lot of new research into phyto-nutrients, which are potent plant compounds that can increase fertility and reduce age-related damage. Eating a wide variety of different coloured foods increases your intake of phyto-nutrients, so aim for a rainbow selection of blue and purple berries, rich green herbs and leafy vegetables, golden turmeric, pink grapefruit, red peppers, orange carrots and apricots and so on.

If you continue to experience problems conceiving, it may also be worth visiting a nutritional therapist to explore any deficiencies, toxicity or imbalances that could be hindering your fertility. Biochemical testing can be very useful to identify potential problems while a tailor-made nutritional programme can help to restore reproductive health in both partners. See the Resources section for more details.

CHAPTER 2

Pre-pregnancy Spring Clean

If you've taken on board the advice to maximise your fertility, then you'll already be on your way to improving your health. Now we're going to look at potential pollutants in more detail and explain how you can minimise exposure, and even eliminate any harmful build-up, to prepare the optimum internal environment for pregnancy.

This is crucial because after nine months in your womb, your baby will be born largely complete, with all the heart, muscle and kidney cells he or she will ever have (as they grow, these cells can only be enlarged). And although the brain, nervous and immune systems will continue to develop, the infrastructure is already established prior to birth.

During this time of rapid development, your baby is therefore extremely vulnerable to any toxins, pesticides and pollution. So limiting your own exposure – and detoxifying what's already accumulated before you get pregnant – is important. Doing this will not only benefit the health of your unborn child greatly, it will also help to improve your own health, appearance and energy levels.

Anti-nutrients in Pregnancy

Good nutrition isn't just about what you eat, it's also about what you don't eat, drink or breathe. Many of the substances considered to be bad for us, like alcohol, pollutants and cigarettes, cause their damage by interfering with essential nutrients. For instance, alcohol depletes vitamin C, vital for cell formation, while lead is a powerful antagonist to zinc and calcium, both crucial for a baby's mental and physical development. These anti-nutrients, perhaps not noticeable in tiny quantities in adults, can have a serious impact on your baby.

Toxic Minerals

After discovering that high lead and cadmium levels and low zinc were associated with stillbirths, difficult pregnancies and deformed babies, Professor Bryce-Smith of the University of Reading began a comprehensive study to determine just how important these minerals are.

His findings, and subsequent research by other scientists, have proved a link between exposure to harmful minerals – such as lead from paint, pollution and petrol (now removed, thanks to Bryce-Smith's campaigning); cadmium from cigarette smoke; aluminium from cookware, baking foil and anti-perspirants; mercury from dental fillings and fish; and even too much copper from water pipes – and birth defects, low birth weight (which is an indicator of poorer health in later life) and developmental problems.

You may think it's unlikely you've got an issue with any of these toxins. But they are all around us and once we are exposed our bodies aren't able to easily get rid of them. Lead, for example, can remain in the body for 20 years or more after initial contact, as a 34-year old client of Susannah's discovered. He hadn't knowingly come into contact with any lead since playing with lead paints as a child. Yet when tested, his lead levels were very high. A three-month detox plan reduced the lead to a safer level and he and his wife went on to conceive a healthy baby boy.

In addition to their toxic effects, these minerals act as antagonists to beneficial minerals and interfere with normal functioning. Cadmium and mercury, for example, deplete zinc, essential for fertility and healthy foetal development.

The other issue is, like many toxins, while we may not notice any obvious effect from exposure as fully grown adults – unless you experience infertility – the effects on a baby in the womb at the most vulnerable stage of development can be far more pronounced, and last for life.

So how do you find out if toxic metals are a factor for you? A urine test or a hair mineral analysis can give an indication of any accumulation. Hair is the easiest to test (unless it's dyed or treated) and the test is relatively inexpensive. It can also give you an idea of your levels of beneficial minerals. However, this test needs to be performed via a nutritional therapist (see the Resources section). Testing both yourself and your partner would normally be included in any preconception consultation.

If high levels of toxic metals are detected, then it's possible with the right diet and supplements to detoxify them and bring your mineral status back into a healthy balance.

Protect Yourself from Pollution

Toxic minerals and pollutants are in the air, the soil and our food. Over the past 100 years, their levels have risen sharply and in many cases, overload the body's capacity to eliminate them. Here's what to do to keep your exposure to the minimum:

- Avoid busy roads and smoky atmospheres where possible.

- Eat organic, wherever possible (see page 20).

- Where you can't eat/buy organic, remove outer leaves of vegetables and thoroughly wash all fresh produce in a vinegar solution (just add a dessertspoon to a bowl of water) to help remove pesticide residues.

- Limit your intake of tuna or non-organic farmed salmon to no more than once a week, if at all, and aim to eat fish from less polluted waters (i.e. Arctic salmon, haddock, hake and sole).

- Opt for stainless steel cookware and don't wrap food in aluminium foil (or if you do, wrap in greaseproof paper first).

- Limit your intake of canned goods, which may be contaminated with aluminium or plastics.

- Cut down on alcohol (and avoid before and during pregnancy), which increases lead and cadmium absorption.

- Avoid antacids as they can contain aluminium salts.

- Avoid refined foods, which lack toxin-fighting nutrients.

- Check if your waterpipes are made of lead or copper (a tell tale sign is blue staining on sinks/baths). If they are, don't use a water softener but do use a water filter.

- Eat sulphur-rich foods to aid detoxification – garlic, onions, leeks and eggs.

- Vitamin C is an all-round detoxifier – eat more strawberries, kiwis, peppers, watercress, citrus fruits and other sources (see page 40) and supplement 1000–2000mg each day.

- In addition, take a good antioxidant supplement (see page 46).

The Case for Organic

More than 31,000 tonnes of pesticides are applied to conventional crops each year in the UK and residues are found on over half of all fruit and vegetables tested. Multiple residues of seven or more different compounds are not uncommon on many foods, and although it's not yet fully known the combined effect of multiple compounds, research suggests they could be hundreds of times more toxic than the same compounds individually.

As well as being particularly damaging to a developing foetus and implicated in miscarriages and birth defects, researchers have linked pesticide exposure with symptoms such as headaches, tremors, lack of energy, depression, anxiety, poor memory, dermatitis, convulsions, nausea, indigestion and diarrhoea. Many pesticides are known or suspected hormone disrupters and experts from the US Environmental Protection Agency rank pesticide residues among the top three environmental cancer risks.

Of the 445 or so pesticides used in conventional farming, only seven of the least harmful (i.e. natural or simple chemical compounds) are allowed in organic farming – and only as a last resort and after consultation with and approval from the certifying body. The routine use of antibiotics – a practice believed to contribute to the development of antibiotic-resistant infections such as MRSA – is banned in organic farming. Eggs, poultry and other meats from organic farms are always free range and animal welfare standards are high. Genetically modified crops and ingredients are also banned (most non-organic

animals providing meat and dairy products in the UK are reared on imported GM-crop-derived feeds). And of the 314 food additives permitted in non-organic food, only a handful from natural sources (such as citric acid from lemons) are allowed in organic foods.

As if these reasons aren't compelling enough for choosing organic, organic produce also contains more nutrients. Artificial fertilisers promote fast growth that swells fruit and vegetables with more water – good news for the farmer (higher yields) but not so good for the consumer (less carrot in your carrot plus more diluted nutrients). A 2001 review published in the *Journal of Complementary Medicine* found that organic crops had significantly higher levels of 21 nutrients analysed compared with non-organic produce. This included 21 per cent more iron, 29 per

cent more magnesium and 27 per cent more vitamin C. Organic spinach, lettuce, cabbage and potatoes showed particularly high levels of minerals.

Research is also now finding that organic produce promotes better health. For example, a Dutch study published in the *British Journal of Nutrition* in 2007 found that where infants and their mothers eat organic dairy foods, the infants suffer a 36 per cent lower incidence of eczema. And animals fed organically grow better, reproduce more successfully and recover faster from illness than those fed on non-organic feed.

Because of the extra resources needed to produce organic food, it understandably costs more. But if you shop wisely, you can limit the impact on your weekly budget. For example, buy local seasonal rather than expensive imported produce. Organic fruit and veg box delivery schemes provide a cost-effective way to do this. Farmers markets sell local produce too, and growing your own is even cheaper. If you have to prioritise, opt for organic meat and dairy, then root vegetables (which tend to have higher pesticide levels), fruit and veg which you don't peel (i.e. apples or tomatoes), grains and finally fruit and veg which you can peel.

Quit Smoking

If you're a smoker you probably realise that smoking is harmful to you, and even more harmful for a developing baby. As well as depleting nutrients and reducing fertility in both women and men, smoking increases the risk of miscarriage and birth defects, along with premature birth and low birth weight, which both mean your baby has an increased risk of ill health in later life. So ideally, aim to quit at least a month – and ideally four months – before you try to conceive. Patrick's book *How to Quit Without Feeling S**t* offers an effective programme to help you reduce then stop smoking without suffering the usual side effects or cravings.

How Much Alcohol is Safe?

If you drink you may wonder whether there's any harm in having the odd glass if you're trying to get pregnant. The problem is that the most vulnerable time is the first few weeks after conception – typically before you even realise you're pregnant. Also, any alcohol consumption can increase your risk of miscarriage.

Figures from the Miscarriage Association suggest that one in every four pregnancies ends in miscarriage. This already high risk more than trebles by drinking just two large (250ml) glasses of wine a week, according to a seven-year study at Denmark's Arhus University. Of almost 25,000 women studied, those who drank five or more units of alcohol a week were almost four times more likely to lose their baby in the early stages of pregnancy. Because the alcohol content in many drinks has increased, a unit is now less than one small (125ml) glass of wine, half a pint of beer or lager, or an alcopop.

Even in successful pregnancies, a baby's brain development and function can be affected by small quantities of drink. Babies exposed to alcohol in the womb have smaller brains with fewer and differently distributed brain cells, and this causes varying degrees of mental deficiency – from mild behavioural problems to obvious mental handicap. Some authorities claim that Foetal Alcohol Syndrome, the official name where damage has been caused by alcohol, is the leading known cause of mental retardation in the Western world. Low birth weight has also been linked to the negative effects of alcohol and studies show there is twice the risk of abnormalities.

So to be safest, avoid alcohol altogether. And if you just can't, limit your intake to just one small glass of wine or beer with food. Again, Patrick's *How to Quit* book offers some effective strategies for reducing dependency on alcohol.

CHAPTER 3
Conception Countdown

We know that a mother's nutritional status at the time of conception, and in first few weeks that follow, is the single most important determinant of a baby's growth in those critical early stages. Following the diet and supplement plan we recommend will help you optimise your nutrient intake. And boosting immune-supporting and libido-enhancing vitamins and minerals can also help to prime you for conception, as will some know-how about timing your baby-making activities! In this chapter we also explain what homocysteine is, and why this naturally occurring substance is a critical marker for a healthy pregnancy.

Immune Power

Catching a virus or infection in the early stages of pregnancy can not only add to the physical stress you are under, but it can also increase your risk of miscarriage or harming your baby at a critical stage in development. So keeping well in the run up to conception is especially important.

We are all frequently exposed to germs and viruses that cause illnesses, but if you have a strong immune system, you're equipped to fight back more effectively and either avoid symptoms of the illness entirely or have a milder attack.

Your immune strength is totally dependent on a sufficient supply of vitamins and minerals. Insufficient intake of vitamins A, B_1, B_2, B_5, B_6, B_{12}, folic acid, C and E suppress immunity, as do deficiencies of iron, zinc, magnesium and selenium. An optimal intake of these nutrients is therefore vital in boosting immune strength.

Since no nutrient works in isolation, it's advisable to supplement a quality high-strength multivitamin and mineral as well as eating an optimal diet – which we outline in Part Two and illustrate in Part Three. Studies have shown that supplementing a multi can also strengthen your immune system and reduce infections.

Extra Help If You Do Become Ill

If you do succumb to an infection or virus while you're trying to conceive or are pregnant (or indeed at any time), there are certain nutrients that can be very effective at helping you fight it off. A nutritional solution is especially advisable at this time because conventional medications can harm your developing baby – research has found that aspirin, for example, can increase risk of miscarriage and impact on a baby's IQ. Even paracetamol, which is considered the 'safer' painkiller, has been linked to cell mutations.

When your body is invaded by an infection, these invaders produce dangerous oxidising chemicals called 'free radicals' that weaken your immune system. Antioxidant nutrients such as vitamins A, C and E plus zinc and selenium disarm these free radicals and turn the tables to weaken the invader. They also have a wide range of other immune-boosting functions. For example, vitamin A helps to maintain the integrity of the digestive tract, lungs and all cell membranes, preventing foreign agents from entering the body, or viruses from entering cells. Vitamin E is another important all-rounder, as it improves immune cell function and is a powerful antioxidant. So if your immune system needs some help, increase your intake of antioxidants (sources are listed in Chapter 5) and supplement with a daily antioxidant formula (see page 46).

In addition, it's worth supplementing extra vitamin C. To date more than a dozen immune-boosting roles of vitamin C have been identified – it helps mature immune cells, improves their performance and is itself anti-viral and anti-bacterial, as well as being able to detoxify toxins produced by bacteria. In addition, it is a natural anti-histamine. However, the dosage of vitamin C is crucial. A review of studies looking at its protective effect against the common cold found that it was only consistently effective in doses of 1000mg or more (almost 20 times the RDA). So we suggest you take at least 1000mg of vitamin C daily, which you can increase to 1000mg an hour if your immune system is under attack. The only word of caution is that large doses of vitamin C can cause loose bowels – but if this happens, just reduce the dose slightly until symptoms subside.

Love Feast

A client of Susannah's reported increased vitality and interest in sex after an initial consultation. 'What's the secret ingredient in that diet or multi you've given me?' she asked. But the only secret was that she was becoming optimally nourished – and so was starting to fire on all cylinders.

The diet and supplement plan outlined in this book will help you to boost your nutrient intake too. And the sooner you make some positive changes, the sooner you'll start to feel perkier. If your libido, or that of your partner, is in need of an extra boost, however, there are some key foods that make an ideal love feast.

First off, research has found that men low in zinc are low in testosterone, have a low sex drive and a low sperm count. A man can also lose up to 3mg of zinc per ejaculation. And for women, a deficiency in zinc can also lead to hormone imbalances which can contribute to low libido. Oysters are the richest known food source of zinc, hence their reputation as a powerful aphrodisiac.

Other sources include fish, meat, eggs, pumpkin seeds, nuts and fresh ginger.

Antioxidant nutrients help to optimise blood flow to sex organs and minimise any damage. Eating a rainbow selection of fruit and vegetables can provide a wide variety of sources – aim for at least six to seven portions a day. An antioxidant supplement will also boost your intake.

B vitamins are needed for testosterone production, adrenal support, making energy and healthy nerves. In particular, vitamin B_1 is needed for healthy thyroid function (low levels of thyroid hormones can impact on sex drive), while B_3 is a vasodilator, enhancing blood flow to sex organs, and is essential for pituitary function, which controls hormone balance. Eating some mushrooms, watercress, cabbage, cauliflower, broccoli, squash, tomatoes, marmite, nuts or seeds daily will increase your intake. And supplementing either a high-strength multi or a B Complex can boost levels further.

Finally, as we outlined in earlier chapters, washing all this lovely food down with a bottle of wine is not advised as alcohol reduces fertility and increases your risk of miscarriage and birth defects. Nor is enjoying an after-dinner coffee, cigar or cigarette for the same reasons. But you could try a cup of ginseng tea, as this Chinese herb is widely regarded as a 'sexual rejuvenator'. Do note, however, that caution is needed with certain herbs in pregnancy, so it's best to stick to teas rather than tinctures or tablets (unless under the guidance of a nutritional therapist or herbalist).

Perfect Timing

In case you didn't know, making a baby isn't quite as easy as just having sex. During a woman's monthly cycle, there is only one day in which an egg is available for fertilisation. However, sperm usually live for three days and under excellent conditions can survive for five. Therefore, if you know when you ovulate, having sex in this five-day window dramatically increases your chances of conception. So, how do you find out when ovulation occurs?

A different type of mucus is produced just before the egg is released – and unlike normal vaginal mucus, fertile mucus is sticky and thread-like, a bit like egg white. It's designed to both nourish and protect the sperm, providing it with channels to move along, thereby increasing its chances of reaching the egg. It's also easy to spot. In a World Health Organisation study, 90 per cent of women could identify their fertile mucus within the first month of learning what to look for.

Another way to tell when you're fertile is by monitoring your resting temperature (i.e. as you wake up in the morning) – this will drop then rise very slightly as you ovulate. There are also ovulation predictor kits that you can buy from chemists and large supermarkets and these measure levels of hormones produced a few days prior to ovulation, although they don't tell you when ovulation actually occurs.

Finally, don't make the mistake of thinking that lots of sex is the answer, or limit sex only to your fertile period. For men, too much sex can reduce sperm concentration and not enough can cause an increase in the build up

Homocysteine: Your Most Important Pregnancy Statistic

If there was some way to test whether you're getting enough folic acid and other B vitamins to prevent common birth defects, or measure how efficient you are at supporting the most critical biological function necessary to ensure your baby's healthy development, would you jump at it? Well such a test exists – and an ever-growing body of evidence supports how important this is for pregnancy.

This test measures your level of a toxic protein in the blood called homocysteine. It's a marker for a critical chemical process in the body called 'methylation' and being a 'good methylator' is what allows you to pass on the best genetic potential and helps cells to divide and grow to full bloom during pregnancy. This biochemical process also helps you make essential substances and break down toxic ones in the body – you methylate about one billion times every second.

Research links high homocysteine levels to infertility and a significantly increased risk of pregnancy problems. In fact, if you have a low level versus a high level you are almost ten times less likely to have a miscarriage, pregnancy complications or a child with a birth defect. Lifestyle choices such as a nutrient-deficient diet and regular coffee or alcohol consumption can increase homocysteine levels. And one in 10 people actually lacks a certain enzyme that keeps homocysteine in check, so predisposing them to higher levels.

The good news is that it's easy to bring down high homocysteine and maintain a healthier low level. How? Well folic acid is part of the story – its ability to lower homocysteine is why pregnant women are advised to supplement it. But it can do this even more effectively if combined with vitamins B_2, B_6, B_{12}, zinc and a nutrient called TMG. Together, and at the right doses, these nutrients can reduce an undesirable homocysteine level – which in pregnancy is anything above 7 – to a healthy level, below 6, in about two months.

You can arrange a test via your doctor (but they'll probably only be willing if you've experienced past pregnancy problems) or a nutritional therapist. You can also do a simple home test that only requires a pinprick blood sample. (See the Resources section for more details.) If your level is above 9, supplement with 1200mcg of folic acid, 1000mcg of B_{12}, 75mg of B_6, 20mg of B_2, 15mg of zinc and 1.5–3g of TMG (see the Resources section for supplement companies). Following the diet outlined in this book will also help to reduce your homocysteine. After three months, retest, and if below 6, resume the standard pregnancy supplement plan recommended in Chapter 6. If not, continue the supplements and retest again in another three months.

of poor-quality sperm. So during your fertile period, every other day is perfect, and once every three or four days the rest of the month.

Incidentally, mapping your fertility is also an effective way to prevent pregnancy while you are getting yourself in prime condition or after giving birth. Of course, you need several cycles to learn when your fertile period occurs, but once this is regular, you then abstain or use barrier methods for seven days prior to your usual ovulation day and for two days afterwards. This way, you can give your body a break from the Pill or coil and clear out any hormone residues. See page 187 for a source of information on natural family planning.

Still Having Trouble Conceiving?

If, after following all the advice in Part One, you still have problems conceiving, we recommend you read our book *Optimum Nutrition Before, During and After Pregnancy* (Piatkus) for more information, then see a nutritional therapist specialising in fertility (see Resources section), or contact Foresight, the preconceptual care charity, for a referral to one of their practitioners. These specialists can work with you and your partner to identify and try to correct any underlying problems such as polycystic ovarian syndrome (PCOS), hormonal insufficiency, parasite or bacterial infections, heavy metal toxicity and food allergies. And it really can work.

A couple in their early 30s, for example, came to see Susannah after 12 months of trying to conceive. They had started to eat more healthily and had given up drinking alcohol but

still no success. After some biochemical tests, Susannah established that they both had high homocysteine levels (see opposite), some key nutritional deficiencies and that the husband had some pathogenic bacteria in his digestive tract. So the couple followed a tailored nutritional programme, avoiding trying to conceive until it was complete and retests were carried out. After three months, their homocysteine was down to a healthy level, their nutrient status improved and the husband's digestion issues were resolved. They then went on to conceive a baby boy after two months of trying, and experienced a healthy pregnancy and a trouble-free natural labour.

Improving your nutrition and addressing any underlying health issues can also help to increase your chances of success if you are planning to try conventional fertility treatment. Foresight statistics suggest the success rate doubles when both partners follow a nutritional protocol.

Some women can conceive successfully but suffer with recurrent miscarriages. Poor nutrition and nutrient deficiencies can be a factor, as can quite common conditions such as thrombophilia and Hughes Syndrome (both of which mean your blood is more likely to clot, which interferes with the baby's early development). Being tested to identify any possible medical issues is important and where a specific condition is present, working with a nutritional therapist can help to correct any imbalance or support the body. For example, reducing levels of the naturally occurring blood compound homocysteine, addressing deficiencies in B_6, B_{12} and folic acid and providing natural blood thinners such as omega-3 essential fats and vitamin E can help to counter-balance thrombophilia or Hughes.

PART TWO

Eating for Two

CHAPTER 4

The Building Blocks of a Healthy Baby

You are what you eat. Every cell in your body – each bone and muscle, your heart, liver and kidneys, every hair on your head – is made from the nutrients you consume. As an adult, it takes seven years to rebuild your entire body. But it takes only nine months to build your baby's from scratch. So getting an optimal intake of all the nutrients you need during pregnancy is paramount.

Of course, you may know of mothers who've eaten a lousy diet and still given birth to a seemingly bonny baby. But medical evidence suggests that babies who have to adapt to a limited supply of nutrients while developing in the womb permanently change their underlying physiology and metabolism. Even if they are born seemingly 'healthy', Professor David Barker from the Medical Research Council Epidemiology Unit at Southampton University has found that these adaptations are the origins of most degenerative diseases in later life.

Mothers who are deficient are also more likely to develop problems during and after pregnancy – for example, poor skin tone and

post-natal depression can be signs of essential fat deficiency.

So let's take a look at the different nutrients you need over the next two chapters, starting with the 'macro' nutrients – that is protein, carbohydrate and fat. The recipes in Part Three then translate our recommendations into delicious meals for you to enjoy.

Eating for Energy

As you'll see in the table opposite, carbohydrate is your body's main fuel source – it provides energy for you to function and energy for your baby to grow and develop. But not all carbohydrates are good news.

The fast-releasing variety – sugar, honey, sweets and most refined foods – provide a sudden burst of energy that gives way to a slump. That's why you can feel tired, irritable or hungry again and crave sweet foods not long after eating a piece of cake or a biscuit. Fast-releasing carbohydrates can also contribute to excess weight gain, which is

The Key Players on Your Plate

PROTEIN
The basic material of all living cells

During pregnancy
Builds your baby's cells and organs
Replenishes your own body's cells

Best sources
Fish, lean meat, yoghurt, cheese, eggs, soya, quinoa (a South American grain), nuts, seeds, lentils, beans, brown rice, broccoli, peas, beans and other seed vegetables

TIP: *Don't rely entirely on animal sources of protein as too many can be too acidic. Enjoy several helpings of vegetable proteins each day too (i.e. nuts, beans, lentils, seed veg).*

CARBOHYDRATE
The body's preferred fuel source

During pregnancy
Energy for your baby's growth and development
Energy for you to feel good and get things done

Best sources
Brown rice and wholemeal pasta, oats, rye and wholemeal breads, beans, lentils, potatoes, quinoa and all vegetables and fruit

TIP: *When you consume too much carbohydrate, it's stored as fat. Sugary sources can also imbalance your energy. So limit your intake of high-sugar and refined (i.e. anything made with white flour) foods.*

ESSENTIAL FATS
The right kinds support brain, hormone and skin health

During pregnancy
Essential fats are needed for your baby's brain and nervous system development, and to keep your hormones in tune, your mood balanced and the skin soft and supple

Best sources
Omega-3: Oily fish such as trout, salmon, anchovies, sardines, herring, mackerel and pilchards. Also in flaxseeds (linseeds) and omega-3 enriched eggs
Omega-6: Flaxseeds (linseeds), pumpkin, sesame and sunflower seeds, walnuts and almonds

TIP: *Seeds make nutritious and energising snacks.*

FIBRE
Keeps things moving

During pregnancy
Supports healthy digestion and clears toxins from your body

Best sources
Oats, oat bran, brown rice, flaxseeds (linseeds), all fruits and vegetables

TIP: *As your pregnancy progresses and your digestive system gets squeezed, increase your intake of oats, veg and fruit to prevent constipation. Note that too many wheat products can irritate the gut.*

something most women want to minimise during pregnancy. This is because your body can only convert a finite amount of carbohydrate into energy at any one time. Any excess is put into storage as fat.

Slow-releasing carbohydrates, on the other hand, do what their name suggests – release their fuel (or sugar) more slowly. This means your food is converted to energy over a longer period of time, providing more sustained energy for you and avoiding the overload that leads to fat storage.

Slow-releasing carbohydrates include whole grains such as brown rice, oats and rye bread, plus vegetables and most fruits. These foods still contain all their nutrients and fibre, which takes longer to digest, whereas refined carbs have the fibre and many nutrients stripped out.

We call slow-releasing carbohydrates low 'Glycemic Load' (or low-GL) foods. They help to stabilise your blood sugar (the level of fuel in your blood to make energy), which regulates your energy and weight.

Fruits such as berries, grapefruit, pears, watermelon, peaches, oranges, plums and apples are all relatively low GL. But the more starchy or sweeter varieties, such as bananas, dates, raisins, dried figs and prunes, contain more sugar, so can imbalance blood sugar if too many are eaten. Fruit juice is also fast-releasing as it's had its fibre stripped out to leave the sugary liquid part. So a better low-GL option is to enjoy fresh fruit whole.

Keeping your blood sugar stable is even more important during pregnancy as your baby requires energy round the clock to fuel its growth. Unlike you, he or she doesn't switch off when you go to sleep. With the exception of some medium-GL treats, the recipes in Part Three are low GL, and include slow-releasing fuel sources, plus protein, which further slows down carbohydrate release and sustains your energy for longer.

Fat Facts: Telling the Good from the Bad

Many people are phobic about fat, believing it to be the cause of weight gain and ill health. But while too many saturated fats found in meat, dairy products and processed foods are bad news, the omega-3 and omega-6 varieties – found in oily fish, nuts and seeds – are essential for the functioning of your body and the healthy development of your baby's brain and nervous system.

Your intake of these 'essential' fats while pregnant has a direct effect on your baby's future IQ. Consuming enough also means you are less likely to develop pre-eclampsia, give birth prematurely or suffer with post-natal depression.

So aim to eat two portions of oily fish a week – but avoid the more polluted large varieties such as tuna or swordfish (generally speaking, the smaller the fish, the less polluted). And snack on a handful of fresh, unsalted nuts and seeds every day. You may also benefit from taking a purified essential fat supplement (see page 46).

For cooking, olive or coconut oils are the best fats for heating, with coconut oil being more stable at high temperatures. Whichever oil you use, avoid browning foods, as this is a sign that the fat is becoming damaged. Once this happens, the structure changes into what's called a trans fat. These are found in fried and processed foods and, along with hydrogenated fats, are worse for you than saturated fat and so are best avoided. During pregnancy, too many trans fats have also been found to reduce a baby's birth weight and lower the quality of breast milk.

For salad dressings and cold sauces, olive oil or nut and seed oils have many health benefits as well as providing great flavour. Aim to buy only cold-pressed nut or seed oils as this helps to ensure the delicate fats they contain aren't heat damaged.

What's Off the Pregnancy Menu?

While eating the right foods is important for your health and that of your baby while you are pregnant, there are also certain foods you should be cautious about.

For starters, some foods carry a small risk of infection and, as your baby is very vulnerable while it's developing, it's recommended you avoid these while pregnant, especially during the first three months.

Avoiding Potentially Harmful Bacteria

Salmonella
- Raw eggs and poultry can harbour Salmonella – in fact it's estimated that as many as 33 per cent of fresh and 41 per cent of frozen chickens are infected – so make sure you cook both thoroughly. For eggs,

this means until both white and yolk turn solid, and avoid buying or having foods made with raw eggs such as sorbet, fresh mayonnaise or chocolate mousse. It is also wise to avoid chilled pre-cooked chicken. Salmonella can cause nausea, diarrhoea and vomiting in the mother, resulting in dehydration which may affect the baby.

Listeria
- Reheat cooked and chilled food (such as leftovers and ready meals) until piping hot.

- Avoid pâté (any kind, even vegetable ones) and soft, mould-ripened or blue-veined cheeses (such as Brie, Camembert, goat's cheese with a rind and Stilton), unless they are made from pasteurised milk or have been thoroughly cooked until piping hot. Soft cheeses like cream cheese, cottage cheese and Mozzarella are all fine, as is feta. Although Parmesan is made from unpasteurised milk, it is generally considered safe to eat during pregnancy as the cheese is too hard for the bacteria to grow. Pre-bagged salads are an ideal breeding ground for Listeria so standard advice is to avoid these. Listeria may only cause mild flu-like symptoms in the mother but can result in miscarriage or stillbirth.

Toxoplasmosis
- Avoid raw or undercooked meat, including Parma ham and salami, in order to ensure that there is no risk of infection from toxoplasmosis, a parasite that can cause complications, particularly in early pregnancy, affecting the baby's developing brain and eyes.

- Toxoplasmosis can also be found in soil, muddy vegetables and cat faeces, so wear gloves when gardening, washing mud-coated vegetables or changing the cat litter (this is a great excuse to delegate this task to someone else).

Raw shellfish and sushi

- Avoid raw shellfish and sushi. Unless really fresh, they can cause serious food poisoning so are best avoided. Sushi can also contain parasites if not prepared properly.

And don't forget basic food preparation rules

- Remember to wash all fruit and vegetables thoroughly (though obviously not those that you peel) to remove any traces of soil or bacteria.

- It's important to cook meat properly to kill off any bacteria but also remember to keep uncooked meat away from any cooked foods in your fridge to avoid cross-contamination. And be sure to wash your hands and utensils thoroughly after preparing meat and don't use the same chopping board as you do for vegetables or bread.

Some More Cautions

Alcohol

Alcohol is also toxic and not safe to your developing baby at any level. We've been advising pregnant women to avoid it for years. Recently, the British government changed its stance to agree with us. Even a few glasses of wine a week can increase risk of miscarriage and cause damage to your baby's brain and nervous system (see page 23 for more on the effects of alcohol).

Coffee and caffeine-containing drinks

As covered in Chapter 1, these can have a negative impact on fertility. But once you're pregnant, many British doctors claim that several cups a day is okay, although anything more may increase risk of miscarriage. However, caffeine crosses the placenta and affects the baby in the same way as the mother – i.e. it increases heart and breathing rate and alters brain activity. And as a growing baby is not yet fully developed, the effects are likely to be more profound. A baby is also less able to detoxify caffeine and it's estimated to stay in their bloodstream for up to 100 hours. Coffee also increases homocysteine, a harmful chemical in the blood (see page 28).

In the US, the Food and Drug Administration (FDA) advises pregnant women to avoid caffeine-containing foods and drugs (and this includes colas) completely. We advise the same. Decaffeinated coffee still contains two other stimulants (theobromine and theophylline) and can be more toxic due to the chemicals used to remove the caffeine. If you want to enjoy the occasional cup, buy an organic variety where the caffeine is removed via the safer 'Swiss water process'.

Green or sprouting potatoes

These contain poisonous substances called alpha-solanine and alpha-chaconine which are linked to increasing spina bifida risk. So be sure you don't eat sprouted potatoes and cut away any green areas before cooking.

Liver

This is often warned against during pregnancy because of its high vitamin A content. However, you do need some vitamin A when you're pregnant (see page 39). So while we don't advise you to stop eating it all together if you enjoy it, we do suggest you limit your consumption to a small portion every other week and eat only organic as this will be less contaminated with the growth hormones, steroids and antibiotics used in conventional farming (the liver being the place all these chemicals get stored). However, if you are eating liver, be sure any supplements you take only contain the vegetable source of vitamin A (beta-carotene) and not any additional animal-derived vitamin A (retinol). This will especially apply to cod liver oil, a very rich source of retinol.

Mercury

Carnivorous fish like shark, marlin, swordfish and tuna can accumulate mercury residues from contaminated waters so are best avoided. If you're a fan of tuna, limit your intake to just once a week. Mercury is a toxic heavy metal that can harm a baby's developing nervous system. Have no more than two portions of oily fish like trout, mackerel, herrings, kippers and sardines per week (salmon and anchovies tend not to be so high in mercury).

Peanuts

The jury is still out on whether peanuts should be avoided or not during pregnancy in order to reduce your child's risk of a peanut allergy. A couple of years ago the received wisdom stated that women with a history of allergies or atopic conditions like asthma or eczema should avoid peanuts (possibly even all nuts completely) due to their strong allergic potential. Then emerging research suggested that avoiding peanuts during pregnancy could in fact sensitise your child! Because she comes from a highly atopic family – but one that doesn't have a history of peanut allergy – Fiona avoided peanuts during pregnancy, but not obsessively so. You must make up your own mind, however, and do whatever feels comfortable. If you do decide to avoid nuts, you'll find that wherever possible, the recipes in Part Three include substitutions, such as seeds. Seeds are from a different family and are far less likely to cause allergies (the one exception being sesame seeds, which fall within the top twelve most common food allergens).

How Much Extra Do I Need to Eat?

While every calorie you eat needs to be nutrient-rich to nourish both you and your baby throughout your pregnancy, it's not necessary to eat for two. In fact, you don't actually need to eat any more until the last three months. And even then it's only an extra 200 calories (the equivalent of an apple and an ounce of Cheddar cheese). The daily calorie guide for the 'average' woman is 2000 calories, increasing to 2200 calories in months seven, eight and nine of pregnancy. Then after you give birth, you'll need an extra 500 calories a day while you're breast feeding (see page 60).

CHAPTER 5
The A to Z of Essential Nutrients

Vitamins and minerals are needed in much smaller amounts than protein, carbohydrate or fat, but they are no less important. These 'micro' nutrients control billions of vital actions in your body every single second of your life, from conception onwards.

For example, the mineral zinc is needed to power more than 100 different reactions, one of which aids fertility and another supports your baby's growth. Vitamin D is essential for strong bones and a robust immune system, which are important to both you and your developing baby. And you probably know that folic acid, a member of the B-vitamin family, is vital for the healthy development of your baby's brain and nervous system.

Vitamins and minerals also help to balance hormones, produce energy, keep your skin clear and healthy, make blood, support the vital work of your organs, trigger muscle contractions, balance mood… They are involved in just about every function of the body.

If you're deficient, your body simply won't work as efficiently as it could. But if your baby doesn't get enough, key organs may not develop properly, resulting in lifelong disability. So let's consider what specific vitamins and minerals do and where you get them from.

Your A to Z of Vitamins and Minerals

Vitamin A

What it does
For baby: vital for growth, plus the development of eyes, skin, organs and mucous membranes. Also involved in proper heart and immune functions.
For you: important for healthy skin, a strong immune system (including protecting against cancer) and night vision.

Best food sources
Liver (organic liver is less polluted, but limit intake to one small piece every other week), carrots, watercress, cabbage, squash, sweet potato, melon, pumpkin, mangoes, tomatoes, broccoli, apricots, papayas, tangerines and asparagus.

Need to know
Vitamin A comes in two forms – retinol (from animal sources) and beta-carotene (from vegetables). Retinol is important for foetal development but can be toxic in high doses. So don't eat too much liver or supplement more than 3000mcg (10,000IU) daily (and none if you are eating liver). As a knee-jerk reaction, any UK supplement containing retinol carries a warning 'not suitable for pregnancy'. But denying yourself any retinol is also not ideal, so just be sure not to exceed 3000mcg a day.

B Vitamins

The family of B vitamins includes vitamins B_1, B_2, B_3, B_5, B_6, B_{12} plus biotin and perhaps the best-known nutrient in pregnancy, folic acid. As explained on page 28, certain B vitamins are key for supporting the vital biochemical process of 'methylation'.

What they do
For baby: key for cell division, which is obviously important in the first few months of pregnancy. Also aid brain and nervous system development and help create new blood cells.
For you: help create new blood cells to accommodate additional volume required in pregnancy. Aid hormone balance, mental function and energy production. Support healthy skin and hair.

Best food sources
Mushrooms, watercress, cabbage, cauliflower, broccoli, alfalfa sprouts, squash, tomatoes (B_1, B_2, B_3, B_5, B_6, biotin); chicken and salmon (B_3); sardines, lamb, eggs and cottage cheese (B_{12}); bananas (B_6); nuts and seeds (folic acid).

Need to know
As B vitamins work in synergy, they are best taken as part of a good multi or B Complex formula that includes 400mcg of folic acid. You may need more than the average recommended doses and a homocysteine test (see page 28) is the ideal way to find out what your individual biochemical requirements are.

Vitamin C

What it does
For baby: assists in the formation of cell membranes and blood vessels.
For you: makes collagen which keeps bones, skin and joints firm. As an antioxidant, detoxifies pollutants and protects against disease. Can also reduce risk of pre-eclampsia, a pregnancy disorder.

Best food sources
Peppers, watercress, cabbage, broccoli, cauliflower, strawberries, lemons, kiwi fruit, peas, melons, oranges, grapefruit, limes, tomatoes.

Need to know
Even the best diet is unlikely to provide an optimal amount of vitamin C, so supplement around 1000mg each day, and more if you are stressed or live in a polluted environment.

Vitamin D

What it does
For baby: aids the formation of bones and tooth enamel (your baby's teeth are already partly formed before birth).
For you: keeps bones healthy, supports your immune system.

Best food sources
Herring, mackerel, salmon, oysters, cottage cheese, eggs. Can also be made in the skin in the presence of sunlight, so sensible sun exposure to arms and face is also advised.

Need to know
The government now recommends pregnant women at risk of deficiency supplement vitamin D. This group includes those with darker skins (who don't synthesise as much in the skin). Aim for 30mcg a day as part of a good-quality multivitamin.

Vitamin E

What it does
For baby: helps transport oxygen to growing cells and protects genetic material from damage. Also assists in the healthy growth and maintenance of the placenta during pregnancy.
For you: protects your cells too and aids wound healing.

Best food sources
Sunflower seeds, peanuts, sesame seeds and other 'seed' foods such as beans and peas, wheat germ, sardines, salmon, sweet potatoes.

Need to know
Vitamin E oil can be rubbed directly on to skin to alleviate marks and scarring (for example after having a Caesarean). Simply cut open a capsule to release the oil.

Vitamin K

What it does
For baby and you: ensures that blood clots when required.

Best food sources
Cauliflower, Brussels sprouts, lettuce, cabbage, beans, broccoli, peas, watercress, asparagus,

potatoes. Vitamin K is also manufactured by beneficial bacteria in the gut.

Need to know
It is not necessary to supplement vitamin K if you have healthy intestinal bacteria. Babies are often given a vitamin K injection at birth in case of deficiency, which in very few cases is linked to internal bleeding. But in healthy mothers who breast-feed, this is not normally necessary.

Calcium

What it does
For baby: a vital component of developing bones and promotes a healthy heart and nervous system.
For you: also necessary for healthy bones, teeth and skin. If there's a deficiency during pregnancy, can increase risk of osteoporosis in the mother in later life.

Best food sources
Cheese, almonds, parsley, corn tortillas, globe artichokes, prunes, pumpkin seeds, cooked dried beans, cabbage, green leafy vegetables.

Need to know
When you're pregnant, your body absorbs more calcium from your diet than normal. But additional supplementation is still advised – what's contained in a good-quality multi is enough for the first trimester, then an extra 300mg (taken with 150mg of magnesium) in the second and third trimesters is recommended.

Chromium

What it does
For baby: helps protect genetic material in cells and is essential for heart function.
For you: helps to balance blood sugar, giving you stable energy and reducing cravings.

Best food sources
Brewers' yeast, wholemeal bread, rye bread, potatoes, wheat germ, green peppers, eggs, chicken, apples, butter, parsnips, cornmeal, lamb chops, Swiss cheese.

Need to know
Can help reduce sugar cravings and aid healthy weight balance. Works in partnership with B_3, so best taken as part of a multi.

Iodine

What it does
For baby: needed for the development of brain and nervous system. Deficiency can lead to hypothyroidism and birth defects.
For you: maintains thyroid function, which is important for metabolism and energy.

Best food sources
Haddock, mackerel, cod, yoghurt, pilchards, plaice, Cheddar cheese, chicken.

Need to know
Most multi formulas designed for pregnant women include iodine, and if you eat fish, you'll get plenty from your diet.

Iron

What it does
For baby: helps support the development of a circulatory system.
For you: supports new blood cell manufacture to accommodate increased volume requirements during pregnancy. Also vital for energy.

Best food sources
Pumpkin seeds, parsley, almonds, dried prunes, cashews, raisins, Brazil nuts, walnuts, dates, red meat, cooked dried beans, sesame seeds, pecan nuts.

Need to know
Iron deficiency (anaemia) is very common in pregnancy. Symptoms include lethargy, pale skin and a sore tongue. Chelated iron supplements are three times more absorbable than iron sulphate or oxide forms commonly prescribed by doctors, which can cause constipation. Vitamin C also aids absorption.

Magnesium

What it does
For baby: works with calcium and vitamin D to form your baby's bones and teeth. It's also key for the development of heart muscles and the nervous system.
For you: promotes healthy muscle function by helping them to relax so is important for labour cramps. Magnesium is also essential for energy production.

Best food sources
Wheat germ, almonds, cashews, brewers' yeast, buckwheat flour, Brazil nuts, peanuts, pecan nuts, cooked beans, garlic, raisins, green peas, potato skin, crab.

Need to know
Magnesium is often called nature's tranquilliser so boosting levels can relieve stress symptoms and aid relaxation. Along with calcium, supplement extra magnesium in the second and third trimester (150mg magnesium to 300mg of calcium).

Manganese

What it does
For baby: helps to form healthy bones, cartilage, tissues and nerves as well as promoting healthy DNA and RNA (our genetic blueprint).
For you: important for insulin production (the hormone that transports glucose from your blood to body cells, where energy is made) as well as brain function and also reduces cell damage.

Best food sources
Watercress, pineapple, okra, endive, blackberries, raspberries, lettuce, grapes, butter beans, strawberries, oats, beetroot, celery.

Need to know
This mineral is often lacking in food so extra is recommended via a multi formula supplement.

Selenium

What it does
For baby: as an antioxidant, it helps to protect against free radicals (toxic by-products of biochemical reactions in our bodies) and cancer-causing substances which can interfere with your baby's development.
For you: reduces inflammation, stimulates your immune system to fight infections and promotes a healthy heart.

Best food sources
Molasses, mushrooms, herring, cottage cheese, cabbage, beef liver (organic liver is less polluted but limit intake to one small piece every other week), courgettes, cod, chicken.

Need to know
Best to supplement as part of a multi or antioxidant formula.

Zinc

What it does
For baby: vital for all areas of growth, promotes healthy nervous system and brain development and aids bone and teeth formation.
For you: aids hormone balance, supports immunity, helps hair to 'bloom' and is essential for constant energy.

Best food sources
Ginger root, lean red meat, pecan nuts, split peas, haddock, green peas, prawns, turnips, Brazil nuts, egg yolk, whole-wheat grain, rye, oats, peanuts, almonds.

Need to know
Research has shown that babies born to mothers who supplemented 25mg of zinc from 19 weeks pregnant had a greater birth weight and head circumference, both of which are indictors for better health (but don't necessarily make giving birth any more difficult!).

Eight Easy Ways to Boost Your Nutrient Intake

1. Eat a multi-coloured variety of fruit and veg to get the best balance of nutrients.
2. Aim to have a salad as a major part of one meal each day.
3. Add fruit to your breakfast and snack mid morning and mid afternoon.
4. Include an extra portion of veg with your evening meal.
5. Buy whole foods (i.e. brown rice, beans, lentils) rather than refined products.
6. Eat as much food as raw as possible. When cooking, steam rather than boil or fry.
7. Wherever possible, buy seasonal organic food and eat it fresh.
8. Supplement your diet with a good multivitamin and mineral formula, plus extra nutrients as needed. When taking supplements make sure that natural sources of vitamins are used, which provide the full complement of other synergistic nutrients.

CHAPTER 6
Supplement Sense

If you're tuned into public health messages, you'll probably know that pregnant women, and those wanting to conceive, should be supplementing their diets with folic acid. This is because this member of the B vitamin family, along with several others, supports a vital biochemical process called methylation which ensures that cells replicate and genetic information is interpreted correctly, so preventing birth defects such as spina bifida. But what about other vitamins and minerals – do you need to supplement these too?

Every survey of eating habits conducted in Britain since the 1980s shows that even those who said they ate a balanced diet fail to get anything like the level of nutrients set in European, American or World Health Organisation Recommended Daily Allowances (RDAs). What is more, the RDAs of vitamins and minerals are set by

governments to prevent deficiency diseases, such as scurvy or rickets, rather than to ensure optimal health. And there is a big difference between a lack of illness and the presence of wellness – and an even bigger difference between the effects of deficiency in you and that of your baby at a crucial time of development.

What's Wrong with the Modern Diet?

Why, you may wonder, does a good diet not contain all the vitamins and minerals we need for health? Studies show us that nutrient levels in food are falling – there are fewer vitamins and particularly minerals in fresh produce today, for example, than in the 1980s. This is partly due to intensive farming on nutrient-depleted soils and also storing 'fresh' food for longer (for instance, oranges may take four to five months from picking to appearing on your supermarket shelf).

Refining food (i.e. turning brown foods into white) also strips away valuable nutrients. In wheat, for example, 25 nutrients are removed in the refining process that turns it into white flour, yet only five (iron, B_1, B_2, B_3 and folic acid) are replaced. On average, 87 per cent of the essential minerals zinc, chromium and manganese are also lost.

In short, we just don't eat what our ancestors ate. A gorilla, for example, often eats more than 1000mg of vitamin C a day – we typically eat less than a tenth of this. And even if we go just a little way back to the Victorians, a recent study in the *Journal of the Royal Society of Medicine* showed they ate far more fruit, vegetables and fish – and the only way to match that nutrient intake today would be to supplement.

The result of a sub-optimum intake of nutrients is a sub-optimum state of health. Most people put up with feeling 'all right' – accepting the odd cold, headache or mouth ulcer and having low energy, poor digestion, depression, etc., as normal. Rates of infertility, miscarriage, pregnancy problems and birth defects are also increasing.

When you are having a baby, getting an optimal intake of all the nutrients you need is vital – not only so that you have a healthy pregnancy but also to ensure that your baby develops to its full potential.

There are now hundreds of scientific studies published in respected medical journals which prove that increasing the intake of vitamins and minerals above RDA levels can reduce birth defects, enhance IQ, improve childhood development, reduce the risk of developing diseases in later years, as well as boosting immunity, alleviating hormonal problems, improving moods, increasing energy and, overall, promoting a long and healthy life. For example, a 1995 study published in the *American Journal of Medical Genetics* found that pregnant women who supplement their diet with a multivitamin reduced the risk of having a baby with a birth defect by a third and cut their risk of a premature or low-birth-weight baby by half.

Your Pregnancy Supplement Plan

To support the nutritional needs of you and your developing baby during pregnancy, a supplement plan to boost levels of vital nutrients is recommended. Vitamin and mineral supplements should ideally also be taken prior to conception as your health during this time is a crucial determinant of your baby's health once conceived. Do note, however, that supplements are no substitute for a good diet, at any time. They are designed, as the name suggests, to supplement the nutrient intake you get from fresh, quality food sources. That's why the diet and recipes in this book are designed to help you maximise your nutrient intake from food as well.

The Basics

To cover the basics, we recommend:

- A pregnancy multivitamin and mineral formula with optimal quantities of all the key nutrients outlined in the table on page 48. This may consist of one, two or even three tablets or capsules a day, which should be taken in split doses (i.e. with breakfast and lunch and/or supper). For guidance see the instructions on your chosen supplement.

- 1000–2000mg of extra vitamin C (an ascorbate formula is better absorbed and tolerated than straight ascorbic acid), again taken in split doses (500mg with each meal).

Optional Extras

- If you don't like fish and seeds, are concerned about pollution in fish or just want to ensure you get an optimal intake of essential fats, take an essential fat formula providing a mixture of both omega-3 EPA/DHA plus some omega-6 GLA (for example, around 400mg EPA, 200mg of DHA and 200mg of GLA). Opt for a product that is purified to ensure pollutants are removed (see the Resources section for suggestions).

- If you are an older mother, live in a polluted environment, are at risk of developing pre-eclampsia or are under a lot of stress, take an antioxidant. A good formula should provide extra beta-carotene, vitamins E and C, selenium and zinc, plus other optional antioxidants such as reduced glutathione, N-acetyl cysteine, co-enzyme Q10 and alpha lipoic acid.

- If you find, after testing, that your homocysteine score is above 9 (see page 28), take a homocysteine-lowering formula that contains 1200mcg of folic acid, 1000mcg of B_{12}, 75mg of B_6, 20mg of B_2, 15mg of zinc and 1.5–3g of TMG. Continue taking until a retest shows your level has fallen below 6.

By the way, you may find your urine becomes yellower. This is a normal by-product of B vitamin metabolism – just drink more water.

Your Supplement Guide

NUTRIENT	SUGGESTED DOSE	BEST FORM (if applicable)
VITAMINS		
A (retinol)	750mcg/ 2500IU*	
A (beta-carotene)	750mcg/ 2500IU	
D	30mcg	Cholecalciferol or Ergocalciferol
E	250mg	D-alpha tocopherol
C	1000–2000mg	Ascorbate or Ester C
B_1 (thiamine)	15–25mg	
B_2 (riboflavin)	15–25mg	
B_3 (niacin)	25mg	Niacinamide
B_5 (pantothenic acid)	25–50mg	
B_6 (pyridoxine)	50mg*	
B_{12} (cyanocobalamin)	25–50mcg	
Folic acid	400–600mcg	
Biotin	50mcg	
MINERALS		
Calcium	200–600mg	Citrate or amino acid chelate
Magnesium	150–300mg	Citrate or amino acid chelate
Iron	10–15mg	Amino acid chelate
Zinc	10–15mg	Citrate, picolinate or amino acid chelate
Manganese	2mg	Citrate, gluconate or amino acid chelate
Chromium	50mcg	Chromium polynicotinate
Selenium	40mcg	Selenomethionine or selenocysteine
Iodine	50mcg	

* A note on safety: the levels of nutrients included in different supplement formulas vary enormously, so use this as a rough guide. Any of the suggested doses are still perfectly safe at double the quantities given. A word of caution on two nutrients, however. Don't supplement more than 3000mcg (10,000IU) of the retinol form of vitamin A (see page 39 for more on this) and don't supplement more than 100mg of B_6 as higher doses may suppress your milk production when you start breast-feeding.

Supplementing Probiotics

Much has been made of the benefits of probiotics and many women wonder if they might be of value during pregnancy. Before deciding if you wish to take them, it helps to understand their role a little better. Each of us is born with a sterile gut, but by the time we reach adulthood, about five pounds of bacteria has taken up residence. The majority of this bacteria are 'friendly' in that they help to break down our food, make certain B vitamins and vitamin K and prevent any nasty bacteria (the bugs that cause food poisoning) from sticking around. However, the balance between friendly and harmful bacteria can sometimes shift in the wrong direction if, for example, you have too many antibiotics, eat a diet high in refined carbohydrates or are under long-term stress. This can cause a variety of digestive problems and can also lead to allergies and related conditions such as asthma and eczema. If you have a family history of any of these, you can help prevent passing them on to your baby by ensuring your gut bacteria is healthy.

The diet recommended in this book will support gut health, supplying plenty of fibre-rich and 'prebiotic' foods that encourage the growth of good bacteria. And research has shown that supplementing your diet with a probiotic – which contains high levels of beneficial bacteria to replenish your gut – can reduce the likelihood of allergies in your baby by 50 per cent. Doing this can also help to prevent your baby inheriting a predisposition to eczema or asthma.

So our advice if you have a history of allergies, eczema or asthma, or have used lots of antibiotics in the past, is to take a probiotic supplement (containing both lactobacillus and acidophilus strains) daily throughout your pregnancy and continue while breast-feeding. See the Resources section for suppliers.

Probiotics can also be helpful if you get an outbreak of thrush (oral or vaginal) and can help to alleviate common digestive problems such as bloating, wind, constipation and diarrhoea. If you suffer with any of these, supplement a high-strength probiotic (look for brands that contain billions rather than millions of live organisms per capsule) until your symptoms have resolved. Natural live yoghurt can also be applied topically for thrush, and is a beneficial food to eat to help to support a healthy gut, but the levels of bacteria are not sufficient to address a specific problem on their own.

CHAPTER 7
Solutions to Pregnancy Problems

Pregnancy can be a demanding time, not only physically but emotionally and mentally too. Following the optimum diet and supplement plan we recommend will equip you to better meet the challenges, but sometimes problems can still occur. Here are some of the more common issues you might encounter, with nutritional strategies to help support you.

Anaemia

Mild anaemia may occur in as many as one in three pregnant women. Symptoms include pallor, tiredness, a sore tongue and a feeling almost as if there's a weight on your shoulders. It's usually the result of a low level of iron in the blood, although deficiencies in B_{12}, folic acid, manganese and B_6 can also cause anaemia.

Your iron levels will be tested throughout your pregnancy and your doctor may prescribe extra if you appear low. Do note, however, that iron in the ferrous form (for example, ferrous sulphate) or as an amino acid chelate is much better absorbed than the ferric form, which

can cause side effects such as constipation. A daily dose of 10–20mg is usually effective, on top of your multivitamin. Higher doses should be used with caution as they can interfere with the absorption of other essential minerals such as zinc.

Eating iron-rich foods (see page 42) will further boost levels, as will having vitamin C-rich foods at the same time, which enhance iron absorption by up to twice as much. So enjoy a glass or fresh orange juice with a boiled egg, or have some seeds or nuts with a piece of fruit.

Backache

The tendons supporting your back become softer in pregnancy due to increased levels of the hormone progesterone. As your baby grows, your centre of gravity is pushed further forwards and, to compensate, many women push their shoulders back and their tummies out, putting strain on their backs. That's why it's particularly important to maintain good posture. Imagine you are held up by a string attached to the top of your head, and keep your shoulders relaxed. When sitting don't slouch, and if you feel you need some support for the lower back, put a cushion between you and the back of the chair. Avoid lifting heavy objects, and when you do lift anything, don't do it by bending over and straining your back muscles. Instead, bend your knees and keep your back straight, taking the weight with your thigh muscles.

If you're really suffering, do consider visiting an osteopath or chiropractor who can assess and help correct any postural compensations that could be causing your discomfort. Pregnancy yoga or pilates can also help to strengthen the back. And having a warm bath with Epsom salts can help to relax tense muscles – buy in boxes from a chemist and add a couple of handfuls to running water before soaking for 15 minutes.

Constipation

Your abdominal organs – stomach, liver, pancreas, bladder and intestines – are already closely packed together, so the arrival of a baby plus placenta, enlarged uterus and fluid leaves little room for expansion. For many women this means a greater chance of constipation since the faecal matter in the large intestine is more compressed and the muscles have less room to keep the contents moving along.

The answer is not to take laxatives but to make sure your diet is especially high in fluids and fibre and low in mucus-forming foods.

Dairy produce, eggs and meat are especially mucus forming and tend to make faecal matter more compacted and harder to pass along. On the other hand, fruits, vegetables, grains, lentils and beans are high in fibre and this fibre absorbs fluid, making the resulting faecal matter light and bulky and easier to pass. The diet and recipes recommended here are all digestion friendly.

It is also a good idea to drink at least 1.5 litres of filtered or bottled water a day (the equivalent of eight glasses), either as it is or in herbal teas or diluted fruit juice. Stirring a dessertspoon of flaxseeds (linseeds) into a glass of water before bed, then drinking the gel-like solution down in the morning, followed by another glass of water, will also help to loosen things up. Taking more vitamin C helps too (1000–2000mg a day), as can taking a probiotic supplement of beneficial bacteria (see page 49).

Cravings

Low zinc levels are associated with the abnormal cravings a pregnant woman often experiences in early pregnancy. In addition, replenishing low iron levels in the body has been successfully used to control abnormal cravings that some women experience for strange, and sometimes harmful, substances such as chalk or coal. Following the optimum diet and supplement plan we recommend should replenish these, but if they persist, see a nutritional therapist who can test your mineral levels (see the Resources section).

Depression

About 10 per cent of pregnant women – and 13 to 15 per cent of new mothers – develop serious depression. But you can do a lot to reduce your risk by being optimally nourished. Two main players in pregnancy-related depression are zinc and essential fats, so try to boost your intake of those.

In a study of 11,721 British women, researchers found that those who consumed greater amounts of seafood (a rich source of both essential fats and zinc) during the last three months of their pregnancy were less likely to show signs of major depression before and for up to eight months after the birth. Those with the highest intakes of omega-3 were half as likely to suffer from depression as women with the lowest. The diet and supplement plan outlined here should ensure your intake of these – and all the essential nutrients – is optimal. If you still feel depressed, aim to supplement an omega-3 fish oil supplement plus 15mg extra of zinc each day. Too much sugar or caffeine can also contribute to blood sugar imbalances that can make you feel low.

Gestational Diabetes

Gestational diabetes is an extreme form of poor blood sugar control (see pages 32–4) where the body is unable to maintain a constant energy level. It usually occurs during the second half of pregnancy and disappears after birth, but it can be an early warning sign of developing diabetes later in life. Your baby may be bigger, increasing the chances of Caesarean delivery, and also has a greater risk of developing diabetes themselves. This condition affects up to three in every hundred women and manifests as a whole host of symptoms including fatigue, irritability, nervousness, depression, poor concentration, excessive thirst, sweating, headaches and digestive problems. If you are diagnosed with gestational diabetes, the diet outlined in this book will help you control it. Specifically:

- Eat complex carbohydrates that release their energy slowly (i.e. rye bread, oats, brown rice, vegetables) and avoid refined carbohydrates (i.e. white bread and pasta, biscuits, cakes) and any foods with added sugar.

- Balance meals and snacks with protein – so eat some seeds and yoghurt with your breakfast cereal or have a boiled egg; make sure main meals include some lean meat, fish, pulses or dairy products; and balance snacks, so have an apple with 10 almonds, hummus and carrot or celery sticks or nut butter on oat cakes, for example.

- Take a multivitamin and mineral to boost nutrient levels, but supplement an extra 200mcg chromium a day specifically to help your body manage glucose. (See the Resources section for suppliers.)

- For more information, read *The Low-GL Diet Bible* (Piatkus), which outlines the best researched diet for reversing and controlling diabetes.

Heartburn

In the last months of pregnancy it's common to experience some heartburn because of the pressure of an enlarged uterus on your stomach. There is no magical cure, other than to avoid the foods that trigger it and to eat small amounts little and often rather than having big meals. You may find it helpful to sleep slightly propped up towards the end of pregnancy. But do avoid antacids as these commonly contain aluminium which is toxic. A quarter of a teaspoonful of sodium bicarbonate (bicarb of soda) dissolved in water and taken between meals can bring relief.

High Blood Pressure

Raised blood pressure commonly occurs in pregnancy and an optimum diet should help to control it. Magnesium can help to lower blood pressure as it helps the artery walls to relax. Supplement 200mg up to three times a day. If this doesn't do the trick, add in 200mg of calcium two to three times a day, plus 1000mg of EPA/DHA fish oil once a day.

Leg Cramps

Cramps are nearly always due to an imbalance of calcium and magnesium. These minerals, as well as sodium and potassium, are called electrolytes because they control the electrical balance that causes muscles to relax and contract. A cramp happens when muscles go into contraction. As a growing baby needs lots of magnesium and calcium to build its bones, pregnant women can often become deficient. So follow the diet and supplement plan we recommend, eat lots of calcium- and magnesium-balanced foods such as green leafy vegetables, nuts and seeds and supplement 600mg calcium with 300mg of magnesium each day. Make sure you also get plenty of fluids as dehydration can make cramps worse.

Morning (Noon and Night) Sickness

During the first three months of pregnancy all the organs of your baby are completely formed. It is during this period – and, of course, before conception – that optimum nutrition is most important. Yet many women experience continual sickness and don't feel like eating healthily. Misnamed 'morning' sickness, the most common signs and symptoms are nausea, usually worse on an empty stomach, and often triggered by smells of certain foods or perfumes; vomiting; aversions to some foods and cravings for others; a metallic taste in the mouth; a feeling of hunger even when feeling nauseous; and relief from nausea by eating.

Surges in hormones and poor blood sugar balance can both contribute to pregnancy sickness. An optimal diet and supplement programme can help to regulate both. But if you still suffer, try the following:

• Always eat breakfast, preferably containing some protein foods such as yoghurt, eggs or a protein-powder smoothie.

- Eat small meals and frequent snacks of fruit and seeds.

- Avoid refined and sugary foods.

- Avoid high-fat junk food containing long lists of additives and preservatives.

- Decrease your intake of dried fruit or undiluted fruit juice, both of which provide concentrated sugar.

- Drink plenty of water between meals.

- Avoid or decrease your intake of coffee and tea.

- Take a multivitamin containing a good level of all the B vitamins and zinc.

- If sickness persists, take 50mg of vitamin B_6 twice a day and 200–500mg of magnesium once a day until the sickness subsides.

- Ginger may also help to relieve the sickness and settle your stomach – take either in capsules or as tea.

Pre-eclampsia

Pre-eclampsia (also called toxaemia) is a condition that only occurs after the fifth or sixth month of pregnancy and affects one in 10 women pregnant for the first time. It is usually caused by a poorly functioning placenta and oxidative stress to the blood vessels. Pre-eclampsia can be difficult to spot as you won't necessarily feel ill – but if it progresses unchecked it can develop into eclampsia, a life-threatening condition where convulsive seizures can occur. The first sign is raised blood pressure which may be accompanied by slight swelling in the ankles. Protein is also present in the urine. Regular check-ups and self monitoring are therefore very important. And following an optimum diet and supplement plan can reduce your risk – research has shown that women who eat more fruit and vegetables and who supplement vitamins B, C and E and essential fats are much less likely to develop the condition.

Stretch Marks

The skin on the abdomen does a remarkable stretching job in pregnancy, but if it expands beyond its elastic capacity, stretch marks can develop. Stretch marks on the stomach, thighs, breasts, hips or shoulder girdle are one of the signs of zinc deficiency, so eating zinc-rich foods such as nuts, fish, peas and eggs, as well as ensuring you get 10–15mg of zinc in your daily supplement, is crucial. Vitamin C is also needed to make collagen, the intercellular glue, and vitamins A and E help to keep skin supple. So make sure your diet provides plenty of these vitamins (see page 39–40 for sources) and again, supplement at the levels suggested (page 48). Applying vitamin E oil (from a vitamin E capsule is best so it's not damaged) or the GLA essential fat oil can also be helpful during the last weeks of pregnancy and after the birth to encourage the skin to contract.

Urinary Tract Infections

Urinary tract infections such as cystitis are more common in pregnancy because higher levels of the pregnancy hormone progesterone can cause your bladder and urinary tract to relax, so urine stays put for longer. As your baby grows and space for your organs constricts, it also becomes harder to fully empty your bladder. Both scenarios make it easier for bacteria to multiply and cause infection. Common symptoms include burning or pain when you pee, urine that's cloudy or contains blood, a more frequent need to pee, lower back pain, a temperature and/or feeling generally grotty.

Drinking plenty of water can help to flush out bacteria before it takes hold, so aim to have the recommended eight glasses a day. Also helpful is limiting your sugar intake (which causes bacteria to multiply) and eating some cranberries or blueberries each day, which contain compounds that help prevent bacteria from adhering to the bladder wall. If you'd rather drink cranberry/blueberry juice, be aware that many brands contain lots of sugar, so look for one that's sweetened with fruit juice (and beware artificial sweeteners that can have many unpleasant side effects). Alternatively, you can buy cranberry powder to make up your own juice. The supplement D-Mannose is another option as this flushes out the common bacteria E-coli – buy from a health food shop and mix with water. Eating plenty of garlic can also help to kill off bacteria (and, if you can bear it, is best eaten raw). From a hygiene perspective, wiping from front to back when you use the loo, washing after a bowel movement, wearing cotton pants rather than g-stings (which can create a bridge for bacteria to travel from your bottom to your urinary tract) and peeing straight after sex can also help to prevent infection.

If you develop an infection, do go to your GP – if left untreated, it can cause pregnancy complications and is more likely to develop into a kidney infection. You may be given antibiotics, and if so, take a probiotic supplement (see page 49) alongside and for a week afterwards to replenish good bacteria levels and reduce your risk of developing thrush.

Varicose Veins and Haemorrhoids (Piles)

Varicose veins and haemorrhoids (piles) are not at all uncommon during pregnancy. They develop because of restricted blood flow and also constipation. All the blood vessels in the feet and legs lead to one big vein in the groin, but if this is compressed by the baby or by a build up of waste matter in the bowel, the blood must return along different routes. This can cause small veins on the surface of the legs to become enlarged, misshapen and swollen, i.e. varicose. Haemorrhoids are varicose veins in the rectal area and often develop due to constipation or sitting for too long.

The secret of avoiding varicose veins and haemorrhoids is to keep your blood vessels in good shape and to minimise the restriction of blood flow. Vitamin C is needed to make collagen which keeps the arteries supple. Vitamin B_3 helps to dilate the blood vessels, while vitamin E and the essential fatty acid EPA thin the blood and help to transport oxygen. All are included in the diet and supplement programme we recommend. Regular exercise will also help to stimulate proper circulation. And eating plenty of soluble fibre – from oats, oat bran, prunes, fruit and vegetables – will keep your stools soft and help you avoid constipation. Also be sure to drink 1.5 litres of fluid each day (from water or herbal teas).

Water Retention

Hormonal changes during pregnancy can mean your body holds on to more sodium and this increases the amount of fluid in your body. So cut down on salty foods (for example, bacon, crisps, canned or processed foods) and boost your intake of potassium-rich foods, such as fruit and vegetables, which help to balance out excess sodium levels. Don't make the mistake of thinking that drinking water will make the problem worse – quite the reverse as it will help to 'flush' out your system, so aim to have two litres a day. Regular exercise will also help to boost lymphatic drainage (your internal cleansing system). And make sure you're not constipated (see page 51) as this will prevent toxins being eliminated and encourage water retention.

Weight Gain

By the end of your pregnancy, your baby may weigh between 3.5 and 4kg (7.7lb and 8.8lb) but you're likely to have gained around 12.5kg (28lbs). Much of this is the placenta, fluid and increase in blood volume that supports the baby, but your body will also store more fat as an energy reserve while your baby is growing and in preparation for breast-feeding.

As a general guide, you're likely to gain about 4kg (8lb) by the end of the first 20 weeks and about a pound per week after that. However, each woman is different. If your weight gain is more, check you are not eating for two (you only need an extra 200 calories a day in the last three months) or filling up on empty calories (i.e. refined, sugary or processed foods) or not exercising enough. The diet and supplement programme we recommend aims to minimise excess weight gain. You could also be suffering from water retention (see left).

If your weight gain is less than half this amount, it is important to check that you are eating enough. Since the more important measure is whether the baby is growing, measuring your waist is a better indication than your weight.

CHAPTER 8
Birth and Beyond

When the time comes, you'll want to be ready for the demands of labour and to recover quickly to enjoy the demands of your new baby. What you eat and the nutrients you take can help you achieve this better. There are also some special nutritional considerations for breast-feeding.

Getting Ready for the Big Event

Two weeks before your due date, stock up on plenty of complex carbohydrates (i.e. whole grains and vegetables) as these are the main energy source for the body to sustain you through labour. You may also want to take a GLA (an essential fat) supplement – 1000mg of starflower or evening primrose oil a day will help you make substances called prostaglandins that prepare your cervix for the birth. Raspberry leaf tea also helps to relax and tone the uterus – so drink several cups a day (you can buy it from health food shops). And if you feel like having sex, semen also contains cervical-toning prostaglandins!

Before you give birth, you transfer a large supply of zinc to your baby to prepare it for life in the outside world. Boosting your intake can replenish this loss, which can enhance your birth recovery rate and reduce your risk of post-natal depression. So if you are not already supplementing, aim to take 15mg of zinc a day for the two weeks before your due date and for two weeks after giving birth.

In terms of energy requirements during labour, giving birth is often compared to running a marathon. After all the good work you have done to create a healthy baby, the last thing you want is to run out of energy and have a prolonged labour that may result in Caesarean delivery and increase your baby's risk of birth-related trauma. So as well as stocking up on complex carbohydrates as outlined above, prepare some energy-boosting supplies to see you through the actual event. Diluted grape juice supplies a readily available source of fruit sugar that should help keep up your energy levels. Avoid caffeinated tea or coffee if offered as this will only lead to energy dips after the initial high. And if you feel hungry, snack on seeds and nuts, oat cakes with nut butter and sticks of carrots or celery.

Your Recovery Plan

Giving birth is probably the most challenging physical process you'll ask of your body – and consequently depletes you of vital nutrient stores. So even if you feel on a 'high' afterwards, it's important to prioritise your own rest and recuperation.

If you have a vaginal birth, you will probably feel sore and bruised. And if you have a Caesarean, you'll need to recover from major surgery with no lifting or driving for six to eight weeks. Whatever your experience, getting the right nutrients can help to speed up the healing process.

Our ancestors and most other mammals found the perfect ready-made solution to replenish all the nutrients lost in labour – eating the placenta! However, while this is still practised in some parts of the world, it is no longer commonplace in Western society. So, if placenta stew doesn't appeal, luckily we have multivitamin and mineral supplements which are far easier to swallow! (See suggested plan outlined on the following page.)

In terms of diet, continue with the healthy meals and snacks you've been eating while pregnant. In particular, boost your intake of iron-rich foods as these will help to replenish your blood after the blood loss that giving birth entails. Aim to eat some pumpkin seeds, nuts, lean meat, prunes and sprinkle food with parsley.

Vitamins A, C and E and zinc are particularly key to repairing damaged tissues, as are essential fats, so make sure you also include foods rich in these nutrients – fresh vegetables and fruit, fish, nuts and seeds are all good sources. These will provide plenty of fibre too – if you're sore down below, you certainly don't want the discomfort of constipation to deal with too! (See page 51 for more on avoiding this).

The amino acid glutamine is particularly effective for mending cuts and wounds, especially after surgery – take 5g (a heaped teaspoon of powder) three times a day 20 minutes before eating (i.e. on an empty stomach) until you've healed. The homoeopathic remedy arnica is also useful for bruising – it's quite safe to take while breast-feeding and is even beneficial to your baby, as its healing properties will be carried in your milk to help him or her recover from the birth too. You can buy this from good chemists and health food shops.

Revitalising Supplement Plan

Up until the birth, you've probably already been taking the supplement plan we recommend in Chapter 6. So, to keep it simple, we've just increased the dosage and added in an antioxidant, if you haven't already been taking one, to boost levels of all the nutrients you need to bounce back to super health. Follow this programme for two weeks then revert to your pregnancy level to sustain you through breast-feeding.

Obviously during this time you'll have a lot on your plate, so we suggest you prepare your 'two week supplement plan' in advance and put each day's supply into 14 small bags or envelopes that you can easily pack into your hospital bag and leave by the kettle to take when you get home.

SUPPLEMENT	BREAKFAST	LUNCH	DINNER
Multivitamin and mineral	I	I	I
Vitamin C (1000 mg)	I	I	I
Antioxidant	I	I	I
Essential fats (EPA/DHA/GLA)	I	I	I
OPTIONAL:			
Glutamine (take before each meal)	5g	5g	5g

See the Resources section at the back for supplier details.

Five-star Milk

The benefits for babies of breast-feeding are multiple – for example, higher IQs, stronger immune systems and a lower chance of developing diabetes, obesity and asthma. Breast-feeding mothers also have a reduced risk of developing breast cancer, heart disease, diabetes, high blood pressure, high cholesterol and osteoporosis. There's also the bonus of losing your baby weight faster, plus being able to eat 500 extra calories a day while feeding. And it's convenient – no making up formulas, sterilising bottles or carting feeding equipment everywhere you go.

However, like acquiring any new skill, breast-feeding successfully can be challenging to begin with, so do seek support to help you get the hang of the technique. Both the National Childbirth Trust and the La Leche League provide local support groups and assistance (see Resources section).

Also be aware that breast milk is only as good as the raw materials used to make it. Eating a great diet and continuing to

supplement are therefore still important – it's just now you are nourishing your growing baby from your breast rather than via the umbilical cord. Key pointers include:

- Ensure you get enough protein, especially if you feel you are not producing enough milk or it's not satiating your baby. Aim to eat a protein food with each meal and snack (for example, eggs, yoghurt, fish, lean meat, pulses, nuts and seeds).

- Drinking lots of liquid is also important to ensure you can produce the volume required. Your baby will be taking between one and two pints of water through your breast milk which needs to be replaced. This means drinking around three litres a day.

- Stress can impede milk flow, so make time to rest and ask for help when you need it.

- Continue to avoid the same foods you did during pregnancy as you can still pass on food poisoning bacteria through your milk.

- Remember that stimulants in coffee, tea, chocolate, cola drinks or any other drink containing sugar or artificial additives will pass into your breast milk too, so are best avoided.

- Aim to eat organic where possible as the pesticides and chemicals will be passed to your baby via your breast milk.

- You can start to drink alcohol again in moderation – but no more than a few glasses of wine, for example, a week. It's best to have it after you've given your baby their last main feed of the day so by the time you give them their night feed, the alcohol will have begun to dissipate. However, if they get colic, hiccups or appear to react, you should stop having any alcohol at all.

For more on breast-feeding, solutions to common baby problems, vaccinations, weaning and establishing healthy eating habits, read our book *Optimum Nutrition Before, During and After Pregnancy* (Piatkus).

PART THREE

The Recipes

Introduction

Of all of the five books that I have co-written with Patrick, I have never felt quite such a personal interest in the subject matter as this one. I recently gave birth to my first child, Oliver, and wrote most of the recipes while pregnant, so I have firsthand experience of the fickle taste buds, the nausea and fatigue, not to mention the excitement and anxiety. I therefore offer the advice and recipes in this section (and the mother and baby product recommendations in the Resources section) with conviction as they are the result of much research for my own benefit as well as yours.

For anyone who is experiencing fertility problems, I sincerely hope that this book will offer practical help and support. I suffered a miscarriage in my first pregnancy and discovered that a genetic blood clotting condition predisposed me to such problems in pregnancy. This hugely traumatic event led me to research the subject in great depth and sparked my desire to write this book. If you have lost a baby or are struggling to conceive, you have my heartfelt sympathy – and I'm delighted that you are taking sensible dietary steps to help optimise your fertility for next time around. If you are already pregnant and are sensibly planning as healthy a pregnancy as possible, then you have my congratulations! In either case, this book is intended to be a useful source of advice and recipes to help you through one of the most significant stages in your life. Please do take a look at the Resources section on page 181–7, where I have included my favourite products and services for the health and wellbeing of mother and baby, all of which come with my personal recommendation.

All of the recipes in this book are safe to eat when pregnant and indeed will positively nourish your body both before and after conception. Patrick and Susannah's advice in Parts One and Two sets out guidance on optimum nutrition before and during pregnancy to maximise your chances of having a healthy baby, but it is worth reiterating the most important dietary requirements briefly:

1. Choose mainly low-glycemic load (GL) foods and drinks (that is, limit sugary foods and drinks and very starchy and refined carbohydrates like white bread and white flour products that will increase blood sugar levels) to maintain blood sugar balance. This can help to reduce morning sickness, tiredness and unnecessary weight gain, as well as lowering your risk of developing gestational diabetes. Most of the recipes in this book are low or medium GL to help make this effortless for you.

2. Eat plenty of fibre-rich foods like fruit, vegetables, whole grains, beans and pulses to aid digestion and reduce the likelihood of constipation and piles during pregnancy.

3. Ensure you are eating lots of folic acid-rich foods like whole grains, green vegetables, beans and pulses to help keep homocysteine levels in check. This increases your chances of conception and reduces the risk of pregnancy complications, as well as promoting proper neural tube development to help protect your baby against deformities.

4. Regularly consume prebiotic foods which feed good bacteria (like onions, garlic, rye, bananas, Jerusalem artichokes, chicory) and probiotic foods (fermented foods like live yoghurt, soya yoghurt or kefir, miso and pickled vegetables) to top up your levels of the good bacteria, which support your immune system and digestion.

5. Eat plenty of essential-fat rich foods (such as oily fish, and to a lesser extent nuts and seeds) to help avoid stretch marks, support foetal brain and eye development and reduce your risk of post-natal depression.

6. Avoid caffeine and alcohol to preserve valuable B vitamins and reduce the load on your liver. This enables it to get on with other essential functions like keeping hormone levels in balance, as well as reducing associated risks during pregnancy – see Part Two page 36 for more information on this.

7. Invest in quality – if you can afford it, increase your food budget to buy better-quality produce while you are trying to conceive and during pregnancy. Local, seasonal produce very often hasn't been subjected to the routine use of pesticides and medication used in more intensive farming methods, and is more likely to contain higher levels of nutrients as it has spent less time travelling. For any organic sceptics, 2007 saw proof at last that organic farming does produce more nutritious food with the largest ever EU-funded study into organic farming, conducted by The University of Newcastle, showing significant increases in nutrient levels in produce grown organically.

Advice Before and During Pregnancy

From personal experience, it is particularly important that you pay attention to your diet before conceiving, in order to be optimally nourished. Once pregnant, you may find, as I certainly did in the earlier stages, that despite your best intentions to eat healthily the nausea, food cravings or food aversions are so strong that you can only face ginger biscuits or similar. In such times your pre-pregnancy stores of vitamins and minerals will become all the more valuable in helping to keep you healthy and able to sustain a healthy pregnancy.

The first trimester is notorious for upsetting your appetite and taste buds. Many women feel ravenous during this time, while others feel too sick to really enjoy their food, or get strange cravings or food aversions that upset the best-laid nutritional plans. At five weeks, when the morning sickness really kicked in, I found myself craving pork pies (not normally on my shopping list!), but as soon as I hit week six just the thought of them made me want to be sick and I found that plain carbohydrate foods like porridge and oat cakes were all that I could manage. By week seven I couldn't face salad and week eight saw me munching on marmalade on toast. I think the best piece of advice for anyone similarly afflicted is to not worry too much. Be reassured that this ghastly phase should pass as you enter the second trimester and the sickness fades. You should have renewed energy levels and be able to face the thought of cooking and eating proper meals

again, which is when this book will really come into its own.

You should find a good spread of recipes in this section so if, as I did, you crave stodge, you can fill up on healthy versions of classic comfort food dishes like the Easy Fish Pie on page 124. Equally, there are plenty of lighter options from Thai-style Fish Balls on page 119 to the Simple Trout Parcels on page 120. If your sweet tooth has been well and truly activated, try the tempting array of Teatime Treats (page 154) and Puddings (page 166) for some healthier versions to appease your sugar cravings. Most of the recipes in this book have a low-GL score to help keep your blood sugar levels balanced but, as I discovered, during pregnancy you may very well crave carbohydrates and your additional energy requirements will mean you feel hungrier; in which case you can simply fill up on bigger portions of any accompaniments like potatoes, rice or pasta. I have also included some recipes that are categorised as medium GL, and a handful of high-GL Teatime Treats and Puddings. Rest assured, however, that although high-GL sweet treats shouldn't feature too often in your diet, the recipes here are far healthier than standard sugary cakes and biscuits, as they focus on nutritious whole grains and fruit plus other natural sweeteners, so they can be enjoyed from time to time as part of a balanced diet.

It is also wise to be aware which foods you should avoid during pregnancy to safeguard against potentially harmful infections. There is much debate over what is safe or not during pregnancy and advice will differ from source to source. Sadly this isn't much help for anyone who is pregnant and looking for definitive advice! Medical advice on the Continent is far more relaxed than in the UK. French women, for example, continue to enjoy soft cheeses and raw egg dishes throughout their pregnancies, seemingly with no noticeable ill effects (although there will be those unlucky few who pick up infections this way). One pregnant friend told me that when she was living in Germany and asked her doctor's advice on what she shouldn't eat during pregnancy, he simply told her not to eat raw chicken! In the UK, however, we tend to be far more cautious – you'll find the recommended precautions in Part Two, pages 35–7. It hardly needs saying but you should also pay particular attention to food hygiene, taking care to wash your hands and utensils thoroughly when handling raw meat and fish to avoid contamination with food poisoning germs like Salmonella and certain strains of *E. coli.*

General Guidance on Recipes

Cook's Notes
Each recipe is accompanied by Cook's Notes, which include instructions on freezing and making in advance plus suitability for vegetarians and allergy sufferers where appropriate – with advice and suggested alternatives on how to make a dish gluten, wheat or dairy free if suitable. Please note that the Allergy Suitability refers to the ingredients within the recipe itself, not to any recommended serving suggestions.

Oven Temperatures
Temperatures given are for standard ovens, so reduce by around 20°C for fan ovens.

Serving Sizes
The serving size of recipes varies according to the particular recipe – some of the breakfasts, for example, only feed one, but can easily be scaled up. Many of the main meals serve more, as even if there are fewer of you eating it, it should last you for a couple of meals afterwards.

Beans and Pulses
I tend to use canned beans and pulses as they are so much easier than soaking and boiling your own, and list canned quantities in the recipes. If you do have the time and inclination to cook your own from scratch, you can simply substitute freshly cooked ones for the same drained quantity of canned beans (a standard 410g can normally contains around 250g drained weight). Dried beans and pulses usually double in weight after cooking, so you would simply half the canned quantity to work out how much to cook. Bear in mind that dried, soaked beans should be adequately cooked, particularly kidney beans.

Black Pepper
You may also notice that freshly ground black pepper appears frequently in the recipes. This is because as well as adding flavour, black pepper contains a substance called piperine that appears to help your body absorb nutrients from food. It is best added before serving rather than before or during cooking however, to avoid damage by heating.

Cooking Oils

Many recipes specify coconut oil or mild olive oil for cooking. This is because these oils are more stable when heated than others. Coconut oil, as well as being very stable when heated, also appears to be readily used for energy rather than being stored as fat. Mild olive oil – that is non-virgin or medium, light, second press olive oil – is better for cooking than extra virgin olive oil, which tends to lose its flavour and health benefits when heated and of course is more expensive. Rapeseed oil is another good choice.

GL levels

As the vast majority of recipes have a low glycemic load to help keep blood sugar levels balanced, they are not marked as such. Where recipes exceed the Holford Diet threshold of 10GLs per meal (for anyone wanting to lose weight prior to conception), the recipe states this in the Cook's notes – i.e. that the dish is medium GL, or, in a couple of instances in the Teatime Treats and Puddings sections, high GL. Although they just tip the scales as high GL, they can certainly be enjoyed as an occasional treat and will help to fill you up if you are pregnant and ravenous (a time when you should not be concerned with dieting unless you are very overweight and following your doctor's advice anyway).

Low-GL Rice

Maharani low-GL rice provides the health benefits of brown rice with the taste and cooking time of white rice. (See Resources for suppliers.)

Sugar Alternatives

The sweet recipes make use of natural sugar alternatives like xylitol and agave syrup, so that you can still enjoy sweet treats but with less of the downsides of sugar or artificial sweeteners. Xylitol is a naturally occurring sugar alcohol sourced from plants, while agave syrup comes from the agave cactus plant (where tequila comes from). Both of them have a very low GL, which means they do not upset blood sugar balance in the way that sugar and standard syrup do. This makes them less fattening and less likely to disturb energy and concentration levels. However, don't view this as a free rein to gorge on sweet things, as they do nothing to discourage a sweet tooth, and excessive amounts of xylitol can upset bowels. Xylitol and agave syrup are used in the same quantity as standard sugar or syrup, although I have also given sugar or syrup options in brackets in case you cannot get hold of them (agave syrup is available in most good health food shops, as is xylitol – see Resources section on page 187 for more information).

Breakfasts

During pregnancy it is common for women to either feel repelled by the thought of food first thing in the morning or absolutely ravenous. During my sister's first trimester she could only face getting up if she munched her way through almost an entire packet of ginger biscuits in bed. Your palette in pregnancy will probably change enormously, but the recipe ideas here are designed to provide something for every taste. If you want a protein-packed, filling breakfast to get you going there are plenty of options such as eggs, equally if you crave sweet things try the delicious Banana Muffins on page 77, which although sweet, are far better than a packet of biscuits as they are full to the brim with whole grain fibre to help your digestion and fill you up, plus potassium to help regulate your blood pressure.

If you are trying for a baby and want to make sure you have a healthy start to the day, these suggestions also provide a plentiful supply of fertility nutrients like protein, B vitamins and zinc. If you usually grab a bowl of sugary, processed cereal, or a coffee and pastry on your way to work, it is worth trying some of the suggestions in this section to set you up for the day and top up your nutrient levels.

Baby-making Breakfast Suggestions

Eggs

Eggs are packed with B vitamins, iron and zinc to nourish you and your baby. Standard advice recommends that you cook the yolks fully to avoid infection while pregnant, so omelettes and fully cooked scrambled eggs are ideal. Serve with wholemeal toast or rye bread for added fibre and minerals. Add flaked smoked salmon or trout for a weekend treat that also provides omega-3 fats to build your baby's brain and help protect your skin from stretch marks. If you don't already, buy organic or free-range eggs as studies have shown that they are far less likely to be infected with Salmonella than battery-farmed eggs.

Beans on Wholemeal Toast

Baked beans are often viewed as unhealthy but in fact they are packed with fibre to help your digestion, as well as protein to fill you up for longer and support your baby's growth. Avoid brands containing artificial sweeteners.

Wholemeal Toast with Nut or Seed Butter

Toast is one of the quickest, easiest breakfast choices. Make it a more nourishing start to the day by choosing wholemeal bread, or perhaps wheat-free rye bread, and top with some form of protein as this helps to slow down the rate at which the bread raises blood sugar levels. For this reason, peanut butter or another nut or seed butter (hazelnut is particularly delicious, from health food stores) is a better choice than jam or honey.

Cereals

Try the Granola recipe on page 74 or, when choosing a shop-bought brand, read the ingredients carefully and choose a whole-grain version that isn't laden with sugar, syrup, honey or sweetened dried fruit. There are plenty of healthy mueslis available these days which do contain the nuts, seeds and whole grains that we recommend, so opt for one of these instead. Try serving them with live natural yoghurt rather than milk for added probiotic bacteria to support the immune system and digestion, and fresh or stewed fruit for natural sweetness plus extra vitamins and fibre. You could also add ground cinnamon and/or ground ginger, both of which provide nutritional value as well as flavour, along with a tablespoon of seeds such as cracked flaxseeds (linseeds) or pumpkin or sunflower seeds.

Fruit

If you don't normally eat breakfast or are suffering from morning sickness during pregnancy, a simple piece of fruit is better than nothing at all. Stir chopped fruit or berries into live natural yoghurt for added protein to make it more substantial, or make a compote by stewing fruit with a splash of water and a little xylitol or sugar to sweeten.

Adding a little cinnamon may help to balance your blood sugar, while a little ground ginger can help to settle nausea.

Smoothies

These are another excellent choice if you cannot face food first thing in the morning. Quick to make and easy to drink, smoothies can easily provide a complete meal in a glass. Blend fresh fruit (or frozen berries when out of season) with live natural yoghurt, which will help your body fight infection and aid digestion. Throw in a tablespoonful of pumpkin seeds for added protein plus zinc, the fertility mineral. Try the Berry Breakfast Smoothie recipe, opposite, or experiment with your own ideas. I always throw in a banana as it helps to thicken the smoothie and gives it a wonderfully smooth consistency. Bananas are also an excellent source of soluble fibre to help your digestion, and have a high potassium content too, helping to regulate fluid levels in the body.

Berry Breakfast Smoothie

This simple, easy-to-fling-together smoothie provides a balanced, nutritious meal in a glass – for those days when you can't face food or are in a rush. It is rich in fibre, protein and key minerals like zinc to nourish you before and during pregnancy. You could use sunflower instead of pumpkin seeds if preferred. If fresh berries are out of season, use frozen ones.

SERVES I

1 banana
3 heaped tbsp (75g/3oz) berries
3 tbsp live natural (or soya) yoghurt
1 tbsp pumpkin seeds
A splash of water, milk or juice

1 Blend the banana, berries, yoghurt and seeds until smooth – some little nibs will remain from the seeds but these are not unpleasant. If you prefer you can blend the seeds up first in a coffee bean grinder or buy ready-ground seeds from the healthy eating aisle of good supermarkets or in health food stores.

2 Add a little liquid to loosen to a drinking consistency. It is best served immediately, but you could add a splash of lemon juice to preserve it to drink later in the day; store chilled.

Cook's notes Allergy suitability: gluten/wheat/dairy free (if using soya yoghurt) • Vegetarian • Can be made in advance

Oat Crunch Berry and Yoghurt Pots

A home-made, healthier (and cheaper) version of the granola yoghurt pots sold in coffee shops and sandwich bars. You can use blueberries, raspberries, other seasonal berries or chopped fruit such as banana or plums. I have used live natural yoghurt rather than the usual high-fat Greek yoghurt, as its probiotic bacteria help the immune system and digestion. The slightly sour tang is also a refreshing contrast to the sweet fruit and crunchy topping, both of which provide fibre and slow-releasing carbohydrates. The topping keeps well so you can make more and store it for quick breakfasts.

SERVES I

Oat crunch topping

1 tsp coconut oil, mild olive oil or butter

1 tsp xylitol (or brown sugar), or to taste

1 heaped tbsp whole rolled oats

1 tbsp mixed nuts and/or seeds (such as flaked almonds, pumpkin seeds and chopped hazelnuts)

1 tbsp wheat germ (optional)

Sprinkle of ground mixed spice, ground ginger or cinnamon

2 tbsp berries or chopped fruit such as banana or plums

100g (4oz) live natural (or soya) yoghurt

1 First make the oat crunch topping. Gently heat the oil or butter in a frying pan and stir in the xylitol or sugar, oats, nuts and/or seeds and wheat germ. Stir for a couple of minutes or so to allow the oats to toast slightly, then season to taste with the spices and set aside to cool.

2 Spoon the fruit into the base of a shallow glass or a small bowl, cover with yoghurt and place the oat crunch on top.

Cook's notes Allergy suitability: wheat/dairy free (if you omit the wheat germ and use soya yoghurt) • Vegetarian • Can be made in advance (chill until ready to eat)

Granola

One survey of granolas showed that most brands contained as much sugar as a chocolate bar! This version is much healthier but tastes just as good thanks to the delicious blend of nuts, seeds and mixed spice, bound together with tahini and agave syrup. Instead of tahini you could use hazelnut butter – it's more expensive and usually only available in health food shops, but it's delicious. Top each bowlful with a tablespoon of dried goji berries or two tablespoons of blueberries or other seasonal berries and serve with live natural yoghurt, milk or a non-dairy milk such as oat or almond milk. Anyone avoiding nuts should simply replace the nuts with more seeds. (Note: the coconut is not a tree nut but the seed of a fruit and so doesn't cause problems for most nut allergy sufferers, although take advice if you are concerned).

SERVES 2 (simply increase the quantities to make up a big batch for easy breakfasts, once you have found your favourite blend of nuts, seeds and spices)

1 tbsp mild olive oil

75g (3oz) whole rolled oats

1 tbsp wheat germ

1 tbsp desiccated coconut

1 tbsp flaked almonds

1 tbsp roughly chopped hazelnuts

1 tbsp pumpkin seeds

1 tbsp sunflower seeds

1 tbsp sesame seeds

1 tbsp cracked flaxseeds (linseeds) or shelled hemp seeds

2 tbsp agave syrup (or honey or golden syrup)

1–2 tbsp dried mixed spice, to taste

1 tbsp tahini or hazelnut butter

1 Preheat the oven to 170°C/325°F/gas mark 3. Line a baking tray with baking paper.

2 Mix all of the granola ingredients, except the dried mixed spice and tahini, together until well combined then spread over the baking tray. Bake in the middle of the oven for 10 minutes to lightly toast.

3 Remove from the oven and stir in the tahini (which helps the mixture to stick together) and mixed spice, to taste.

4 Leave to cool then store in an airtight container.

Cook's notes Allergy suitability: dairy/yeast free • Vegetarian • Can be made in advance

Cinnamon Porridge with Wheat Germ and Seeds

Porridge is renowned for its filling, warming qualities, making it an excellent breakfast choice. Its high soluble fibre and water content also mean that it will soothe and ease digestion and reduce your risk of constipation – and the even less mentionable, but just as common, pregnancy complaint of piles. Sprinkle the porridge with zinc-packed pumpkin seeds and wheat germ (an excellent source of the baby-making vitamin folic acid, plus vitamin E to nourish your skin and help protect against stretch marks). Agave syrup provides natural sweetness with far less impact on blood sugar levels than ordinary sugar and syrup. Alternatively, use Manuka honey, which is safe to use in pregnancy, is very soothing and healing to the stomach and digestive tract, and is antibacterial.

SERVES 1

4 heaped tbsp whole porridge oats
1 heaped tbsp wheat germ
1 tbsp pumpkin seeds or other seeds
1 tsp ground cinnamon or ground mixed spice, or to taste
1 tbsp agave syrup or Manuka honey

1 Place the oats in a pan and add two parts water to one part oats.

2 Slowly simmer, stirring, until the oats thicken and absorb the water.

3 Pour into a bowl and sprinkle the wheat germ, seeds and cinnamon or mixed spice on top then drizzle with the agave syrup or honey.

Cook's notes Allergy suitability: dairy/yeast free • Vegetarian

Banana Muffins

This sweet, filling muffin will help to ease sugar cravings and keep you going for a few hours at least. It is a far better option than a coffee shop muffin, which is likely to be heavily sweetened and made from refined white flour. This recipe is very simple and is bursting with bananas, which provide natural sweetness and fibre; and potassium to help regulate fluid levels. You can use a non-dairy milk like oat, rice or almond milk as an alternative to milk. The sunflower seeds sprinkled on top provide crunch plus vitamin E and omega-6 fats to help protect your skin. They could be replaced with pumpkin seeds (or omitted entirely).

MAKES 8–10 MUFFINS

75g (3oz) butter, softened (or coconut oil or dairy-free margarine suitable for baking)

50g (2oz) xylitol (or soft brown sugar)

2 large or 3 medium bananas

120ml (4fl oz) semi-skimmed milk (or oat, rice or almond milk)

2 medium free-range or organic eggs

1 tsp vanilla extract

150g (5oz) plain wholemeal flour

1 tsp baking powder

1 tsp bicarbonate of soda

50g (2oz) dried mixed fruit or raisins

25g (1oz) sunflower seeds

1 Preheat the oven to 180°C/350°F/gas mark 4. Grease eight to 10 muffin cases and place in a muffin tray or on a baking sheet.

2 Cream the butter (or coconut oil or margarine) and xylitol (or sugar) together until soft and creamy.

3 Blend or mix in all of the remaining ingredients, except for the dried fruit and seeds, until smooth. If you are doing this by hand, it is easier to mash the bananas separately.

4 Stir in the dried mixed fruit and spoon two heaped tablespoons of mixture evenly into each of the muffin cases. Sprinkle the tops with sunflower seeds.

5 Bake for around 25–30 minutes or until the tops are starting to turn golden and are fairly firm to the touch, then remove from the oven and rest in the tray for five minutes. Remove the muffins from the tray and finish cooling on a wire rack. Store in an airtight container.

Cook's notes Allergy suitability: dairy free (if using dairy-free margarine or coconut oil and dairy-free milk) • Vegetarian • Can be made in advance • Suitable for freezing

Scrambled Eggs with Watercress on Soda Bread

Wholemeal soda bread makes an absolutely delicious base for scrambled eggs. This recipe makes two loaves as soda bread is easy to make and freezes well, but to save time you could buy a loaf. Pregnant women are advised to cook eggs thoroughly so don't serve your scrambled eggs too runny. Watercress not only provides a peppery flavour but is a rich source of vitamin C.

SERVES 1 (with plenty of bread left over!)

Wholemeal soda bread
450g (1lb) wholemeal flour
1/2 tsp sea salt
2 tsp baking powder
1 tsp bicarbonate of soda
1 dessertspoon soft brown sugar
300ml (1/2 pt) mixture of milk and water
1 tbsp plain natural yoghurt

Scrambled eggs
Good knob of butter
2 large free-range or organic eggs, beaten
Sprinkle of sea salt
Freshly ground black pepper
Handful of watercress, roughly chopped

1 Preheat the oven to 220°C/425°F/gas mark 7 and grease a large baking tray. Put the flour, salt, baking powder and bicarbonate of soda in a food processor and blend for 10 seconds to combine.

2 Dissolve the sugar in the milk and water mixture and add to the dry ingredients along with the yoghurt. Process for 10 seconds then scrape the sides and blitz for five seconds to thoroughly blend the mixture. If the mixture is not quite firm, gradually add another tablespoon or two of flour to the mixture, keeping the motor running as you do so, until the dough leaves the sides of the bowl clean.

3 Take the dough out of the bowl and shape into two round, fairly flat loaves (like large buns). Place the loaves on the baking tray, leaving as much space as possible between them, and cover each one (or both together, if they will fit) with a large, ovenproof bowl, leaving enough space for the loaves to rise. Bake for 30 minutes.

4 Remove the bowls, return the loaves to the oven to bake for a further 10 minutes then allow to cool for 10–15 minutes.

5 To make the scrambled eggs, gently melt the butter in a saucepan and pour in the eggs. Put the toast on at this point.

6 Slowly stir the eggs with a wooden spoon, scraping along the base of the pan as they cook to keep them moving and help stop them sticking. Remove from the heat as soon as the eggs are almost set but still a little runny/moist as they will carry on cooking in the pan. Season to taste.

7 Place the toasted soda bread on a plate, cover with watercress and then top with the scrambled eggs.

Cook's notes Vegetarian

Omelette

Omelettes are a good choice during pregnancy as both egg yolks and whites are fully cooked, removing any concerns over food poisoning. They are an excellent source of protein to keep your own strength up and to act as the building blocks for your baby. They also provide zinc – a key fertility mineral for both women and men. You can vary this basic omelette recipe to include ingredients like diced smoked salmon (in which case you don't need to add as much salt) or ham, tomato and cheese, or fried mushrooms.

SERVES 1

2 medium or large free-range or organic eggs
Good pinch of sea salt
1 tbsp mild olive oil, coconut oil or butter
Freshly ground black pepper

1 Beat the eggs and salt together in a bowl.

2 Gently heat the oil or butter in a small frying pan then pour in the beaten egg. Slowly stir the mixture for a few minutes as it sets, pulling it from the edges of the pan and into the middle as it cooks so that all of the egg mixture is exposed to the heat on the base of the pan.

3 When the base has coloured and set, carefully fold the omelette in half and let sit for a half a minute or so just to cook the middle before easing it out of the pan and onto a plate. Sprinkle with black pepper and eat immediately.

Cook's notes Allergy suitability: gluten/wheat/dairy free (if using oil not butter)

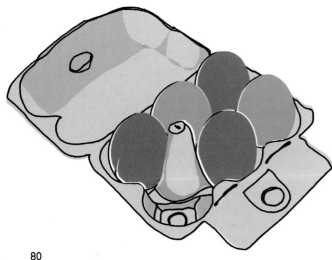

Snack Attacks

Energy levels unsurprisingly can plummet during pregnancy and it can be incredibly difficult to withstand the lure of the biscuit tin. Even if you are not yet pregnant, you may, like many women, suffer from imbalanced blood sugar levels and rely on sweet, refined foods and drinks to get you through the day. This is undesirable in terms of your energy, concentration levels, mood and weight. Such quick-fix snacks contain negligible goodness and are often termed 'anti-nutrients' as they contribute precious few nutrients, yet they can use up your own stores of vitamins and minerals during processing by the body, leaving you worse off. If you feel your energy levels dropping and need to snack between meals, try to choose a healthier option, such as those listed here, or perhaps one of the Teatime Treats on pages 154–65 for a healthier alternative to standard cakes and biscuits. If your resolve weakens, don't beat yourself up unduly but it is worth remembering that your baby's taste buds will be influenced by your own during pregnancy and breast-feeding. So get them off to the best possible start and reduce their likelihood of having a sweet tooth or struggling with blood sugar balance by limiting your own sugar intake. A high sugar intake also increases your likelihood of developing gestational diabetes – all the more reason to choose your snacks with care.

Fruit

There is good reason for eating your five a day; a piece of fruit (with live natural yoghurt or a handful of nuts if wished) will top up your levels of fibre, water and enzymes to help your digestion. The vitamin C fruit contains supports your immune system and aids collagen production to keep your skin looking youthful, not to mention the phytonutrients (plant nutrients) fruit contains to help keep you healthy. Fresh fruit is generally better than dried fruit, which is a concentrated source of fruit sugar – but still miles better than a bar of chocolate if you need a sweet fix.

Smoothie

Ideally blend your own smoothies to get maximum benefits from the vitamins, antioxidants and enzymes contained in fresh produce – some of which are destroyed when bottled smoothies are pasteurised. Add some water, milk or unsweetened, live natural yoghurt to loosen the consistency if necessary. You can also add a tablespoon of seeds – such as pumpkin or sunflower seeds, or a blend of all of these – for additional protein, minerals and essential fats. See the Berry Breakfast Smoothie on page 71 and the Drinks section on page 175 for more ideas.

Wholemeal Toast or Oat Cakes

Wholemeal bread provides all of the goodness of the grain, including fibre and folic acid, which reduces the likelihood of your baby developing neural tube defects during early pregnancy. Rye bread and oat cakes are also a good wheat-free choice, making them easier to digest. Top your bread with a protein-rich spread such as nut or seed butter as this helps to steady the energy release to fill you up for longer. If you are a Marmite (yeast extract) fan, you will be pleased to hear that this is an excellent source of B vitamins, particularly B_{12}, a vitamin that vegetarians and vegans can easily become deficient in and which helps to keep homocysteine levels in check – of particular importance during pregnancy.

Brown Rice Cakes

Puffed rice cakes are not such a good energy source as wholemeal bread or oat cakes as they are very quickly broken down into simple sugar, so they don't fill you up for as long. They are, however, very easy to eat if your stomach feels sensitive. They got me through many a draining business trip when I was first pregnant. Made from brown rice, they are also rich in B vitamins. Top with cottage cheese, hummus, hard-boiled eggs or nut or seed butter for added protein to make them more filling.

Olives

Olives are rich in heart-friendly monounsaturated fats and are a little known source of iron and vitamin E. They are a much better choice than crisps if you crave salty food. Avoid ones which have been dyed black (they will list E numbers on the back) in favour of green or naturally dark olives like Kalamata.

Corn on the Cob

This was one of my favourite early pregnancy foods. Corn on the cob is very rich in fibre and B vitamins, particularly vitamin B_5 or pantothenic acid, which plays a key role in energy production. Cover in boiling water and simmer, covered, for up to ten minutes, depending on how soft you like your corn. Let it cool a little then eat with your fingers as is, or dot with a little butter or drizzle with extra virgin olive oil and a pinch of sea salt and/or paprika.

Avocado

Avocados are rich in potassium, which helps to regulate blood pressure, plus this delicious fruit is an incredibly rich source of antioxidant carotenoids and tocopherols, and the high fat content actively helps your body absorb these carotenoids. Eat it plain or sprinkle with a little lemon juice, sea salt and freshly ground black pepper.

Hummus

Hummus is a good source of slow-releasing carbohydrate and protein to fill you up for longer. Beans and pulses like chickpeas also contain hormone-balancing substances called phyto-oestrogens, making them a useful addition to the diet of anyone with hormone-related fertility issues. Try our Pine Nut and Sun-dried Pepper Hummus recipe on page 97, or grab a pot from the deli or supermarket and eat with oat cakes and crudités.

Smoked paprika nuts

This is another good snack for anyone who would normally be munching on peanuts and crisps. It contains plenty of protein and valuable minerals like magnesium (excellent for relaxing the mind and body when under stress) and zinc (needed for reproduction and for avoiding stretch marks), while still providing a delicious salty, spicy flavour. Make a big batch as they keep for ages (ideally store in a glass jar, somewhere dark).

400g (14oz) mixed nuts
1–2 tbsp mild olive oil
1 tsp smoked paprika
Sea salt

1 Preheat the oven to 170°C/325°F/gas mark 3.

2 Place the nuts in a bowl and drizzle with enough of the oil to lightly coat the nuts when stirred. Sprinkle with the smoked paprika (or ordinary paprika if you don't have smoked) and a little sea salt then stir to coat evenly. Spread over a baking tray.

3 Roast at the top of the oven for around 15 minutes, shaking the tray to turn them over halfway through, or until they just start to colour and toast slightly.

4 Taste and adjust the seasoning if necessary – you can add more paprika and salt after cooking. They're delicious when still warm or cooled.

Cook's notes Allergy suitability: gluten/wheat/dairy/yeast free • Vegetarian • Can be made in advance

Light Meals

Whether you want a light lunch or a starter, there are plenty of delicious dishes to choose from in this section. Try the Tapenade, Smoked Trout and Watercress Rye Sandwich on page 91, which is packed with the omega-3 essential fats vital for foetal brain and eye development, not to mention for your own skin; the Pine Nut and Sun-dried Pepper Hummus on page 97 or the delicious Pea and Ham Soup on page 88, which can be made in bulk for easy, filling meals in minutes. The emphasis here is on quick, simple dishes that you can throw together with the minimum of fuss but still enjoy great tasting, healthy food. I'm sure that these recipes will become everyday staples before, during and after pregnancy.

Many women find that at some point during their pregnancy the baby takes up so much room that they cannot eat as much at one sitting as they normally would. In which case, smaller meals like the recipes in this

section make sense. If you do suffer from heartburn or similar digestive complaints, try slowing down the pace at which you eat to give your tummy more time to process each mouthful. Easier said than done I know – I am guilty of wolfing down my food most of the time.

Creamy Leek and Almond Soup

This dead-easy soup tastes far nicer than the simple ingredients would suggest. The addition of the almonds serves to thicken the soup as well as contributing valuable protein and calcium – both of which are important during pregnancy. You could substitute non-dairy milk and use oil instead of butter to make this dairy free, although I don't think the flavour or consistency is nearly as good.

SERVES 4–6

1kg (2.2lb) leeks
Large knob of butter
350g (12oz) ground almonds
1.1L (2pt) vegetable stock or bouillon
1.1L (2pt) semi-skimmed milk
Freshly ground black pepper
Sea salt

1 Trim the ends off the leeks – but use as much of the green tops as possible. Rinse and roughly slice.

2 Heat the butter in a large saucepan or stock pot and sweat the leeks for a minute to coat. (If you wish, reserve a few slices as a garnish.)

3 Add the almonds and cook gently for a few minutes, stirring. Add the stock or bouillon to the pan, bring to the boil then reduce the heat and simmer, covered, for around 15 minutes.

4 If you are freezing the soup, cool and freeze at this stage. Otherwise, add the milk and blend with a hand-held blender until very smooth then season to taste.

Cook's notes Allergy suitability: gluten/wheat free (depending on the contents of the stock or bouillon) • Vegetarian • Can be made in advance • Suitable for freezing

Pea and Ham Soup

Try this old-fashioned winter soup if you are craving crisps and other heavily salted foods; the ham provides so much salty flavour that there is no need for separate seasoning or even to add stock. You could also use a ham hock instead (around 250g/9oz) if you can get hold of one (soaked in water overnight if necessary to remove the excess salt). It is very important to soak the peas overnight in a large pan of water first, rinse them well and boil them rapidly for 10 minutes in order to make them digestible. This is a very filling meal in itself, although it is also delicious with a slice of wholemeal bread or the Spelt and Seed Bread on page 143. It can be easily batch cooked and frozen for meals at a later date.

SERVES 3–4

1 large or 2 small leeks, sliced

2 celery sticks, sliced

1 tbsp mild olive oil

250g (9oz) green split peas, soaked overnight and rinsed

250g (9oz) smoked gammon or bacon bits

1 bay leaf

5 sprigs fresh thyme

Freshly ground black pepper

1 Sauté the leeks and celery in the oil in a large saucepan for a minute or two then cover to let the vegetables steam-fry inside for around five to eight minutes more to soften. This method preserves more nutrients than simple sautéing in an open pan.

2 Add the split peas, ham, 1.1L (2pt) water and the herbs and bring to a rapid boil, uncovered, for 10 minutes. Skim off the worst of the scum that forms on the surface. Reduce the heat and simmer, covered, for a further hour to an hour and a quarter, until the split peas have softened and the ham is falling off the bone if using a hock.

3 Remove the ham hock if using and pull off the meat; tear into small pieces or roughly dice (discarding the bones and very fatty bits). Reserve to add back to the soup after blending for a chunky texture, or throw the pieces into the pan to blend along with the soup.

4 Blend the soup using a hand-held blender until fairly smooth. Add plenty of freshly ground black pepper and taste to check the flavour – the meat should provide enough salt without the need to add extra.

Cook's notes Allergy suitability: gluten/wheat/dairy/yeast free • Medium GL • Can be made in advance • Suitable for freezing

Spiced Butternut Squash Soup

This mildly spiced soup is satisfyingly thick and very soothing for sensitive stomachs. It has a natural sweetness from the roasted squash and a rich, creamy texture from the coconut milk. Don't buy reduced-fat coconut milk as coconut fat contains a beneficial fat called lauric acid, which helps support your immune system as it is antiviral and antibacterial. In addition, coconut fat is made up of special plant-based saturated fats which appear to be readily burned as energy rather than being stored as fat.

SERVES 4

1kg/2.2lb butternut squash
2 tbsp mild olive oil
1 tbsp curry powder (as hot as you prefer)
2 leeks, sliced
1–2 tsp mild olive oil
300ml (1/2pt) vegetable stock
400ml can coconut milk
1/2 tsp sea salt, or to taste
Freshly ground black pepper

1 Preheat the oven to 200°C/400°F/gas mark 6.

2 Cut open the squash, scrape out the seeds and cube the flesh (unpeeled for added fibre). Place the cubes in a bowl, sprinkle over the 2 tablespoons of oil and the curry powder and toss to coat. Spread the cubes over a baking tray or roasting tin and roast for around 50 minutes, turning halfway through.

3 Meanwhile, sauté the leeks in the remaining oil in a large saucepan for a few minutes to soften (put the lid on after sautéing for a minute to steam-fry them and preserve more nutrients).

4 Add the stock and coconut milk to the pan and, when ready, add the roasted butternut squash. Blend until smooth or your preferred consistency – you can add more stock to thin the soup if you prefer. Season to taste then bring up to temperature before serving, if necessary.

Cook's notes Allergy suitability: gluten/wheat/dairy/yeast free (depending on the stock content) • Vegetarian • Can be made in advance • Suitable for freezing

Lentil and Carrot Soup

This filling soup is mildly spiced with the warming flavours of cumin and coriander which, along with the high fibre content, aid digestion. It's very quick and easy to make. You could also throw in a handful of chopped parsley and coriander if wished, before serving with hunks of Spelt and Seed Bread (see page 143) or wholemeal rolls.

SERVES 4

2 tbsp mild olive oil
2 garlic cloves, crushed
2 red onions, diced
2 tsp ground cumin
4 tsp ground coriander
200g (7oz) red split lentils
6 medium carrots, finely sliced
1.1L (2pt) hot vegetable stock
A little sea salt, to taste
Freshly ground black pepper

1 Heat the oil in a saucepan and gently sweat the garlic and onion with the cumin and coriander for around five minutes to soften the onions.

2 Add the lentils and carrots to the pan and pour in the stock. Bring to the boil then simmer, covered, for around 20–30 minutes, until the lentils have completely softened, stirring occasionally to prevent the soup from sticking.

3 Blend using a hand-held blender until smooth then season to taste.

Cook's notes Allergy suitability: gluten/wheat/dairy/yeast free (depending on the stock content) • Vegetarian • Medium GL • Can be made in advance • Suitable for freezing

Tapenade, Smoked Trout and Watercress Rye Sandwich

This full-flavoured open sandwich makes an interesting change if you are sick of more standard sandwich fillings. If you cannot get hold of hot-smoked trout use hot-smoked salmon instead (hot smoking simply means that the food is smoked directly over a fire to give it a firmer, flakier texture: standard smoked salmon is cold smoked). Equally, the dish would work well with pastrami or good-quality ham. The vitamin C-rich watercress makes this a real skin booster, as does the omega-3 in the oily fish, both of which help keep skin soft, supple and youthful looking. The omega-3 fats are also essential for brain and eye development in your baby.

SERVES 2

2 thin slices pumpernickel-style rye bread
1 tbsp tapenade (or pesto)
1 hot-smoked trout fillet
Handful of watercress, roughly chopped
Squeeze of fresh lemon juice
Freshly ground black pepper

1 Toast the rye bread and spread each slice with the tapenade or pesto.

2 Flake the fish, checking for bones as you do so.

3 Sprinkle the chopped watercress evenly over the bread then place the flaked fish on top.

4 Squeeze a little lemon juice over each sandwich, sprinkle with black pepper then cut in half and serve.

Cook's notes Allergy suitability: wheat/dairy free (unless using pesto) • Vegetarian • Can be made in advance

Roasted Sweet Potato, Avocado and Pumpkin Seed Salad

This wonderfully colourful dish can either be served as a generous side salad or as a vegetarian main meal. The different colours offer a range of different phyto-nutrients; plant nutrients which have specific health benefits such as fighting infection and inflammation. The herbs in the dressing can be varied or use any dark green leaves such as watercress, rocket or spinach. Choose an unwaxed lemon to avoid potentially harmful waxes and pesticides.

SERVES 2

1 medium sweet potato
1 tbsp mild olive oil
2 good handfuls rocket
2 good handfuls baby leaf spinach
225g (8oz) cherry tomatoes, halved
1 ripe avocado
1 tbsp pumpkin seeds, toasted if you prefer

Dressing
A handful each of flat-leaf parsley and basil
2 tbsp extra virgin olive oil
Good pinch of sea salt, or to taste
Freshly ground black pepper
Zest of 1/2 an organic or unwaxed lemon
1 tbsp lemon juice, or to taste

1 Preheat the oven to 200°C/400°F/gas mark 6.

2 Cut the unpeeled sweet potato into long, evenly sized wedges, place them on a roasting tin, drizzle with the oil and toss to coat. Roast for 35 minutes.

3 Meanwhile, very finely chop the parsley and basil (or blitz in a food processor) and mix with the rest of the dressing ingredients. Adjust the seasoning to taste.

4 Toss the rocket, spinach and tomatoes together and place in a salad bowl or on two plates.

5 Peel, stone and slice the avocado and spread over the mixed leaves. Top with the sweet potato wedges, scatter with the pumpkin seeds then finally spoon the dressing generously over the top.

Cook's notes Allergy suitability: gluten/wheat/dairy/yeast free • Vegetarian • Can be made in advance (roast the sweet potatoes and make the dressing in advance but don't slice the avocado or construct the salad until just before serving)

Extremely Lazy Antipasti Salad

This simple dish has become a favourite of ours as it is so quick to fling together but tastes fabulous – and it combines some very nutrient-dense ingredients. It is ideal during the first trimester if, like me, your energy levels hit the floor and you don't feel like either preparing or eating heavy meals. When buying an avocado, look for one with a bottle neck rather than a round shape, as this indicates that it has been tree-ripened and will have more flavour. Serve this salad with crusty wholemeal bread or toasted wholemeal pitta bread.

SERVES 2 (or can be easily doubled up to make a sharing platter for friends)

4 handfuls of salad leaves, such as spinach, rocket and watercress

¼ of a red onion, very finely slivered

1 ripe avocado

2 large, ripe tomatoes, finely sliced

3 tbsp artichoke hearts in olive oil, roughly chopped

3 tbsp sun-blush tomatoes in olive oil, roughly chopped

100g (4oz) buffalo mozzarella ball, drained

Drizzle of good-quality salad dressing

Small handful of basil leaves

Freshly ground black pepper

1 Put the salad leaves on a large plate or platter and scatter the onion slices on top.

2 Stone the avocado, slice the flesh lengthways then scoop out with a spoon and lay over the leaves.

3 Place the tomato slices on top then scatter over the artichoke hearts and sun-blush tomatoes.

4 Tear the mozzarella into rough strips, or slice fairly thinly, arrange on top then drizzle the salad with a little dressing. Finally, sprinkle with basil and black pepper.

Cook's notes Allergy suitability: gluten/wheat free • Vegetarian

Noodle Salad

A simple but oh-so-delicious noodle salad that was born out of store cupboard and fridge staples. It has come to be a popular lunchtime favourite in my house, particularly as it is eminently adaptable to suit various ingredients. Try julienned carrots or peppers and finely shredded white cabbage and spring onions instead of the vegetables here, or cashew nuts instead of sesame seeds. Fresh root ginger may help to alleviate morning sickness and is also good for helping to fight infections. The sprouted seeds are packed with enzymes and antioxidants for a real nutrient boost – you can grow them at home or buy them from health food shops, or simply use cress.

SERVES 2

90g (3¹/₂oz) soba or brown rice noodles

410g can chickpeas, rinsed and drained

¹/₂ a red onion, finely diced

¹/₂ a large cucumber, julienned

2 ripe tomatoes, diced

1 tbsp peeled and grated fresh root ginger

2 heaped tbsp sprouted seeds such as broccoli or alfalfa

2 good handfuls of baby leaf spinach or watercress, finely chopped

3 tbsp sesame seeds

Dressing

Juice of a lime (or lemon)

A good drizzle of tamari soy sauce or soy sauce, or Thai fish sauce, to taste

A good drizzle of toasted sesame oil, to taste

1 Cook the noodles according to the pack instructions then place in a mixing bowl.

2 Add the rest of the salad ingredients and toss well to mix thoroughly.

3 Season to taste with the dressing ingredients.

Cook's notes Allergy suitability: dairy/wheat/gluten free (if using 100 per cent buckwheat soba noodles – many brands add wheat so check the label; gluten or wheat free if using tamari soy sauce – check that it is not from fermented barley if you cannot tolerate gluten) • Vegetarian • Can be made in advance (keep chilled and serve at room temperature)

Chickpea, Chilli and Feta Salad

Light, refreshing and full of bite, this salad is very easy to throw together and extremely tasty. The chickpeas contain fibre and slow-releasing carbohydrate to fill you up for longer, as well as phyto-oestrogens which have special hormone-balancing properties. For anyone who is unsure, feta cheese is safe to eat during pregnancy. Serve this salad on its own for a light lunch or with toasted wholemeal pitta bread, a slice of Spelt and Seed Bread (see page 143) or Pine Nut and Roasted Pepper Corn Bread (see page 144).

SERVES 2

410g can chickpeas, rinsed and drained

3 ripe tomatoes, or 10 cherry tomatoes, diced

1/3 of a cucumber, diced

8 spring onions, finely sliced

2 tsp finely chopped mild red chilli, deseeded

Juice of 1/2 a lemon, or to taste

Freshly ground black pepper

100g (4oz) feta cheese

1 Place the chickpeas in a large bowl and stir in the tomatoes, cucumber, spring onions and chilli.

2 Season to taste with the lemon juice and black pepper.

3 Crumble the feta cheese on top and gently fold in. Don't over-mix the salad or add the feta earlier as it tends to disintegrate and turn the whole salad a milky colour.

Cook's notes Allergy suitability: gluten/wheat free • Vegetarian • Can be made in advance

Pine Nut and Sun-dried Pepper Hummus

Chickpeas are rich in fibre and hormone-balancing phyto-oestrogens. This version of the classic Middle Eastern dip is given a Mediterranean flavour by the pine nuts and sun-dried peppers (you'll find these in jars in the deli or supermarket). Making your own hummus allows you to control the oil content and avoid the E numbers added to some cheaper brands. For a light meal, serve it with salad and wholemeal bread or the delicious Pine Nut and Roasted Pepper Corn Bread on page 144.

SERVES 2

410g can chickpeas in water, rinsed and drained

Juice of $1/2$ a lemon, or to taste

1 large garlic clove, crushed

1 tbsp tahini

75ml (2$1/2$fl oz) extra virgin olive oil

1 tsp sea salt, or to taste

50g (2oz) sun-dried or roasted peppers in olive oil, drained

2 tbsp pine nuts

1 Blend the chickpeas, lemon juice, garlic, tahini, oil (use more or less depending on the consistency preferred or use some of the drained oil from the sun-dried peppers) and salt together in a food processor until smooth and creamy.

2 Add the peppers and pine nuts and blend again to combine (I like to leave a slightly coarse texture), then taste and adjust the seasoning and the consistency with more lemon juice, oil or salt if desired.

Cook's notes Allergy suitability: gluten/wheat/dairy/yeast free • Vegetarian • Can be made in advance (keeps well for a couple of days in the fridge)

Sun-dried Tomato and Pine Nut Stuffed Peppers

These soft, roasted peppers are bursting with Mediterranean flavours and make a delicious light vegetarian lunch. They are very easy to prepare and can be made in advance. The recipe is also a good way of using up any leftover cooked rice from a previous meal (100g/4oz cooked rice equates to 50g/2oz dried weight). (Always remember that cooked rice should be heated thoroughly to prevent food poisoning). Onions and garlic contain sulphur, which accounts for their strong smell but which has very beneficial health properties, helping to maintain a healthy immune system and aid liver detoxification. Brown basmati rice has a very low glycemic load so it provides longer lasting energy and doesn't upset blood sugar levels. Serve with dark green leaves like rocket, spinach and watercress, or little gem lettuce leaves.

SERVES 2

2 large red peppers
1/2 tbsp coconut oil or mild olive oil
1 medium red onion, finely chopped
2 garlic cloves, crushed
150g (5oz) mushrooms, cleaned and sliced
100g (4oz) brown basmati rice (or 'low-GL' rice), cooked
1 tbsp pine nuts (or pumpkin seeds if you are avoiding nuts)
6 large pieces sun-dried tomato, finely chopped
1 tsp Italian mixed dried herbs, herbes de Provence, or oregano
Handful fresh basil leaves or baby leaf spinach, chopped
A little sea salt, to taste
Freshly ground black pepper
A handful of fresh basil leaves

1 Preheat the oven to 200°C/400°F/gas mark 6.

2 Cut the peppers in half lengthways through the stalk, then remove the seeds and trim the membranes.

3 Heat the oil in a frying pan and gently sauté the onion and garlic for a couple of minutes. Add the mushrooms and fry for a further three to five minutes to soften.

4 In a large bowl, combine this mixture with the cooked rice, pine nuts, sun-dried tomatoes, herbs and basil or spinach. Season with a little salt and black pepper to taste.

5 Stuff the peppers with the mixture, pressing down to squash as much in as possible. If you are preparing them in advance, store in the fridge until ready to cook (or you can also cook them in advance and serve at room temperature).

6 Place on the baking tray and bake for 25–35 minutes or until the peppers look fairly soft. Serve sprinkled with the basil leaves.

Cook's notes Allergy suitability: gluten/wheat/dairy free • Vegetarian • Can be made in advance

Main Meals

Whether you are a confirmed carnivore or a vegetarian you will find lots of main meal ideas in this section. There are plenty of meat and fish recipes to choose from – with particular attention paid to oily fish dishes to help you to consume adequate omega-3 fats for your baby's brain and eye development. There's also an array of vegetarian options using a variety of nutritious ingredients to provide sufficient protein for you and your baby. In fact, these main meals have been purposefully designed to supply all of the eight essential amino acids which make up what we call 'complete protein'. That is, they provide the raw materials for all of your protein needs, which include the production of neurotransmitters to help your brain to process information, and support liver detoxification – particularly important for anyone trying to improve their chances of conceiving. And of course if you are already pregnant, protein is vital for your baby's growth and development.

These meals have also been designed to be low or medium GL to ensure that they do not raise blood sugar levels unduly. This will help you maintain good energy and concentration levels and a good mood, and avoid undue weight gain. You can make them as substantial as you wish, according to your appetite, by serving with a large portion of accompaniments such as potatoes or rice, although for anyone watching their weight or monitoring blood sugar balance,

do bear in mind that this will affect the overall GL score of the meal.

If your energy levels flag at the end of the day and the prospect of cooking is unappealing, be assured that the recipes here are quick and simple, to make it easy for you to throw together a nutritious meal. Dishes like the Thai-style Fish Balls on page 119 or the Lamb Burgers with Avocado and Mixed Bean and Tomato Salad on page 114 can be prepared in minutes. Others, like Chicken and Puy Lentil One Pot on page 102, may take a little longer to prepare but can be left to their own devices once cooking, and cook in one pot to limit washing up. You can also make a large batch so that you have easy meals to chill or freeze for a later date.

Meat and Poultry

If you are confused about whether meat is good or bad, or whether you should be eating red or white meat, free range or organic, there are no hard and fast rules. In general, meat can be a very nutritious part of a balanced diet. Red meat's reputation in particular has suffered in recent years with the fad for low-fat diets. In fact, the fat content depends on the cut and quality of the meat. Outdoor-reared beef can be far leaner than battery chickens which have no room to exercise. Plus, the *type* of fat is affected by the animal's diet and living conditions. Intensively reared animals tend to have far higher levels of saturated fat than traditionally farmed ones which get more exercise and more natural feed. So, if like me you love meat, there is no need to give it up for health reasons, simply make sure that you buy the best-quality meat that you can afford. Another top tip is to eat it with plenty of fibre-rich vegetables to aid in its digestion.

The recipes in this section include a good range of leaner cuts and types of meat such as venison, which is naturally very low in fat, for example in the Venison Sausages Braised with Red Wine, Rosemary and Sage on page 111 and chicken thighs in the Tomato and Basil Chicken Patties on page 104. As far as accompaniments go, you'll find plenty of fibre-rich vegetable side dishes to choose from on pages 142–53.

During pregnancy, make sure you cook all beef, pork and lamb until medium to well done in order to ensure that there is no risk of infection from toxoplasmosis, a parasite that can cause pregnancy complications, particularly in early pregnancy.

I became something of a carnivore during my pregnancy, even developing a love affair with pork pies for a short while. Although these certainly can't be recommended on health grounds, I think that the high levels of minerals, such as iron and zinc, not to mention the ready source of protein, makes meat a useful food during pregnancy.

Chicken and Puy Lentil One Pot

Puy lentils are the only type of lentil to hold their shape once cooked, avoiding the mushy consistency that puts many people off these highly nutritious pulses. They make an interesting change to potatoes to thicken this casserole and help to fill you up. As well as containing fibre and protein, lentils are also a significant source of magnesium and folic acid. This rich, filling stew is a complete meal on its own but you may like to serve it with some steamed Savoy cabbage or spring greens and Sweet Potato Mash (see page 146) to help soak up the delicious sauce.

SERVES 4

16 shallots or 4 large red onions

2 tbsp coconut oil or mild olive oil

4 garlic cloves, crushed

250g (9oz) button mushrooms, left whole

4 tsp ground coriander

4 tsp ground cumin

1 tbsp grated or finely chopped fresh root ginger

8 tbsp tomato purée

2 carrots, thinly sliced

2 celery sticks, sliced

1.1L (2pt) hot chicken stock

200g (7oz) dried Puy lentils

4 large chicken thighs or 8 small thigh fillets, skinned

Freshly ground black pepper

A little sea salt, if required

1 Peel the shallots and leave whole (a fiddle to peel, but they look great if you are serving this to guests) or slice the onions into wedges (much simpler). Heat the oil in a large, lidded saucepan or stockpot and add the onions, garlic and mushrooms. Sauté gently for around five minutes then stir in the coriander, cumin and ginger and cook for a couple of minutes more.

2 Stir in the tomato purée and add the carrots and celery, stock, lentils and the chicken to the pan. Stir to ensure that the chicken is submerged in the liquid then cover.

3 Simmer for 35 minutes then uncover and simmer for a further 15 minutes or so more, as necessary, to let the sauce thicken and the chicken cook through – test a piece to see that the juices run clear.

4 Season with black pepper then taste to check the flavour; add a little sea salt if you like.

Cook's notes Allergy suitability: gluten/wheat/dairy/yeast free (depending on the content of the stock) • Can be made in advance • Suitable for freezing

Chicken Cacciatore

There are a million different ways to make this classic Italian dish, which literally translates as Hunter's Chicken, but I have come up with a quick and easy version for minimum effort but great flavour. You can use eight chicken thighs or four chicken breasts if you prefer. Serve with wholewheat pasta or baked potatoes and salad or steamed broccoli or other greens if wished.

SERVES 4

4 chicken legs with thighs
A little sea salt for sprinkling
3 tbsp mild olive oil
2 garlic cloves, crushed
1 red onion, chopped
250g (9oz) mushrooms, sliced
2 x 400g cans plum tomatoes, chopped
2 bay leaves (optional)
2 tsp dried oregano, or to taste
A little sea salt, to taste
Freshly ground black pepper

1 Sprinkle the chicken pieces with a little salt. Heat two tablespoons of the oil in a large frying pan, add the chicken and fry for around five minutes until golden on each side. Do them in batches if necessary, in order not to overcrowd the pan. Transfer the cooked pieces to a large saucepan.

2 Add the remaining oil to the frying pan and sweat the garlic, onion and mushrooms for around eight minutes to soften.

3 Place the onion mixture in the saucepan with the chicken. Add the canned tomatoes (including juice) and herbs. Bring to the boil then reduce the heat, cover and simmer for around 30 minutes, or until the chicken is cooked through and tender (the juices should run clear), stirring to turn the chicken and coat it in juice from time to time. Remove the lid for the second half of cooking to let the sauce reduce.

4 Season to taste and remove the bay leaves before serving.

Cook's notes Allergy suitability: gluten/wheat/dairy free • Can be made in advance • Suitable for freezing

Tomato and Basil Chicken Patties

These Mediterranean-flavoured patties use thigh meat rather than breast, as dark meat tends to contain more zinc, iron, B vitamins and protein than white meat. It is also, of course, considerably cheaper than buying chicken breasts, and I agree with Asian chefs who feel that it has more flavour. The patties are delicious served with the Quinoa with Roasted Vegetables on page 149 and a simple rocket or baby leaf spinach salad. Alternatively, treat them as burgers and stuff in a wholemeal roll or wholemeal pitta bread, with lettuce, tomato and cucumber.

SERVES 4

8 skinless, boneless chicken thigh fillets

2 large garlic cloves, crushed

1 small red onion

100g (4oz) sun-blush tomatoes in olive oil, with 2 tbsp of their marinating oil

2 good handfuls fresh basil leaves

1 tsp sea salt

Freshly ground black pepper

50g (2oz) pine nuts (omit to make this nut free)

1 Preheat the oven to 180°C/350°F/gas mark 4. Lightly grease or line a baking tray.

2 Put the chicken, garlic, onion, sun-blush tomatoes and oil, basil, salt and plenty of pepper into a food processor and blend until the mixture is very finely chopped and well combined. Alternatively, if you do not have a blender you could finely chop the ingredients by hand and mix together. This will give a coarser texture.

3 Shape into eight large (or 16 smaller) patties, flatten slightly then sprinkle the pine nuts over the top, if using, before placing on the baking tray. Pop in the oven to cook for around 25 minutes, or until the meat is cooked through (the juices should run clear).

Cook's notes Allergy suitability: gluten/wheat/dairy/yeast free • Can be prepared in advance • Suitable for freezing

Beef and Barley One Pot

I absolutely craved stodge while pregnant with Ollie. If, like me, you become obsessed with carbohydrate-laden comfort food, try this delicious one-pot meal. The red meat provides plenty of iron to help flagging energy levels and stave off anaemia – a risk in late pregnancy – and the barley is suitably filling and high in fibre and minerals.

SERVES 4

Mild olive oil

450g (1lb) braising steak, cut into bite-size cubes

2 onions, sliced

250g (9oz) mushrooms, sliced

4 carrots, sliced

1 bay leaf

1L (1³/₄pt) beef stock

300g (11oz) pot or pearl barley (if using pot barley, soak for six hours or overnight)

A small glass of red wine

Freshly ground black pepper

Sea salt, to taste

1 Preheat the oven to 150°C/300°F/gas mark 2.

2 Heat a little oil in a frying pan, add the beef and brown on all sides, in stages. Transfer to a casserole dish when done.

3 Add the onions and mushrooms to the casserole dish along with the carrots, bay leaf, stock and barley.

4 Pour the wine into the frying pan and bring to the boil to reduce, scraping off the sediment as you stir. Pour over the meat and vegetables in the casserole – the meat should be almost completely covered.

5 Place the lid on the casserole and cook in the oven for around two to two and a half hours, stirring halfway. You can always add more stock if the barley absorbs all of the liquid and you prefer more of a stew-type sauce. Season to taste before serving.

Cook's notes Allergy suitability: wheat/dairy free (depending on the contents of the stock used) • Medium GL • Can be made in advance

Pork and Shiitake Mushroom Stir-fry

Shiitake mushrooms have been used medicinally in the East for centuries and, more recently, they have been found to contain immune-supporting properties. This highly flavoured Chinese-style stir-fry is a healthier alternative to a Chinese takeaway, providing lean protein and iron from the red meat along with antioxidants and fibre from the vegetables. Serve with brown rice or noodles.

SERVES 2–3

3 tbsp unsalted cashew nuts (omit to make nut free)

Mild oil for frying like rapeseed

450g (1lb) pork mince

125g (4¹/₂oz) shiitake mushrooms, sliced

2 carrots, thinly sliced on the diagonal

2 tbsp tamari (wheat-free soy sauce) or soy sauce

4 spring onions, finely sliced on the diagonal

3 tbsp hoisin sauce

1 Toast the cashew nuts (if using) in a dry wok or frying pan for a few minutes to colour then roughly chop and reserve.

2 Heat a little oil in the pan and fry the mince for a couple of minutes to brown then reserve.

3 Add a little more oil to the pan and stir-fry the mushrooms for a few minutes until softened and coloured.

4 Throw the carrots into the pan along with the tamari or soy and stir-fry for a further three or four minutes or so to soften slightly.

5 Finally, add the reserved nuts and pork along with the spring onions and hoisin sauce and stir-fry for a further couple of minutes until everything is golden and coated.

Cook's notes Allergy suitability: dairy/gluten/wheat free (depending on soya or tamari sauce)

Jambalaya

This traditional Cajun one-pot dish can feature any kind of meat or seafood from chicken, sausage, ham, pork or prawns, making it ideal for using up leftovers. I like to use boneless, skinless chicken thighs as they are easy to prepare and the dark thigh meat is higher in helpful minerals like iron than chicken breast.

SERVES 4

Mild olive oil
500g (1lb 2oz) chicken or pork, cubed
4 tsp Jerk seasoning
2 onions, sliced
2 garlic cloves, crushed
2 red peppers, deseeded and thinly sliced
200g (7oz) smoked sausage, sliced
1L (1³/4 pt) pork or chicken stock
300g (11oz) brown basmati rice
180g (6oz) cooked tail-on jumbo prawns
Handful of flat-leaf parsley, chopped
Freshly ground black pepper

1 Heat the oil in a large, lidded saucepan and brown the chicken or pork for several minutes to colour on all sides then remove from the pan and reserve.

2 Add the Jerk seasoning, onions, garlic and pepper to the pan (along with a little more oil if necessary) and fry for five minutes or so to start to soften the vegetables.

3 Stir in the sausage and fry for a further couple of minutes to colour slightly then add the browned meat and pour in the stock. Bring to the boil then add the rice.

4 Reduce to a simmer, cover and cook for about 45 minutes, by which time the rice should be cooked and the liquid absorbed (stir halfway through the cooking time and check to see whether or not all the liquid has been absorbed by the rice – if necessary, add a little more stock or some water). Three to four minutes before the end of the cooking time, add the prawns and parsley and stir through. Season and serve.

Cook's notes Allergy suitability: gluten/wheat/dairy free (depending on the contents of the stock) • Can be made in advance

Sausage, Olive and Vegetable Bake

A simple but filling supper that combines Mediterranean vegetables with British bangers (use sausages with a high meat content – around 80 per cent). The bright colours of the vegetables are a good indicator of the dish's high phyto-nutrient content – the peppers, onions and tomato purée are positively bursting with antioxidants to help keep you and your baby healthy. You can use any combination of red, yellow or orange peppers and, if you prefer, replace the courgettes with an additional two peppers. Serve with baked or new potatoes, mash, or with the Roasted Celeriac on page 152.

SERVES 4

2 peppers, sliced into long, thin strips

2 courgettes, sliced into long, thin wedges

2 red onions, sliced into thin wedges

2 garlic cloves, finely sliced

100g (4oz) pitted Kalamata olives, drained and roughly chopped

300g (11oz) tomato passata

2 tsp dried oregano

Good pinch of sea salt

8 good-quality sausages

Freshly ground black pepper

Freshly torn basil leaves to garnish (optional)

1 Preheat the oven to 190°C/375°F/gas mark 5.

2 Place the sliced vegetables in a large, shallow casserole dish and stir in the garlic, olives, tomato passata, oregano and salt. Lay the sausages on top and cook for around an hour or until the sausages are golden and cooked and the vegetables are soft, turning the sausages halfway through to colour on both sides.

3 Season with black pepper and scatter torn basil leaves (if using) over the top before serving.

Cook's notes Allergy suitability: dairy free • Can be made in advance

Venison Sausages Braised with Red Wine, Rosemary and Sage

Venison is incredibly lean and a very rich source of B vitamins and iron, both of which are important for energy production. You could easily substitute normal sausages, however, just choose ones with a high meat content (around 80 per cent). Serve with Sweet Potato Mash (see page 146) or a baked sweet potato to help mop up the rich sauce. If you are pregnant and concerned over your alcohol intake, don't worry about the red wine in this recipe – the alcohol will be cooked off.

SERVES 4 (leftovers make for an easy meal the next day)

2 tbsp mild olive oil
12 venison sausages
4 large garlic cloves, peeled
500g (1lb 2oz) shallots, peeled, or red onions
6 celery sticks, thickly sliced on the diagonal
400g (14oz) chestnut mushrooms, quartered
420ml (14fl oz) hot beef stock
600ml (1pt) red wine
4 carrots, sliced
1–2 tbsp chopped fresh rosemary leaves
1–2 tbsp chopped fresh sage leaves
1–2 tbsp cornflour (optional)
Freshly ground black pepper
Sea salt, to taste

1 Heat the oil in a casserole dish or large frying pan. Add the sausages and cook them for eight to 10 minutes until they are evenly coloured. Browning them thoroughly at this stage is crucial to avoiding them looking grey and limp in the finished casserole. Also, take care not to split the skins by turning them over too soon. Transfer to a plate.

2 Sweat the garlic, shallots (or use red onions to save time fiddling around with peeling), celery and mushrooms in same pan for around five minutes.

3 Return the sausages to the pan and add the beef stock, red wine, carrots, rosemary and sage. Bring to the boil and simmer very gently, covered, for around 30 minutes then remove the lid and simmer, uncovered, for another 20 minutes or so to reduce the liquid.

4 If you need to thicken the sauce, mix the cornflour with two to four tablespoons of cold water until smooth and add to the pan, stirring for a couple of minutes to let it come to the boil and thicken the sauce. Season with pepper and taste – add salt if needed.

Cook's notes Allergy suitability: dairy/gluten/wheat free (depending on the sausage content) • Can be made in advance

Lamb and Butternut Squash Casserole

This delicious, warming casserole makes good use of Middle Eastern spices like cumin, cinnamon, ginger and turmeric to provide flavour and also help make it easier to digest. Serve a big bowlful on its own or with steamed greens or cabbage and mashed or baked potatoes or sweet potatoes to mop up the delicious juices.

SERVES 2

1 tbsp coconut oil or mild olive oil

250g (9oz) diced lamb fillet

1 red onion, sliced

1 leek, sliced

1/2 a butternut squash (350g/12oz), unpeeled, seeds scraped out and cubed

1/2 tsp ground cumin

1/2 tsp ground cinnamon

1/2 tsp ground ginger

1/2 tsp turmeric

500ml (17fl oz) lamb stock (or a mix of beef and chicken)

1 tbsp cornflour

Freshly ground black pepper

A little sea salt, if necessary

1 Preheat oven to 170°C/325°F/gas mark 3.

2 Heat the oil in a large saucepan or hob-proof casserole dish, add the lamb and brown it on all sides for around four minutes to seal. Stir in the onion, leek, squash and spices.

3 Pour in the stock, stir then cover and place in the oven for an hour.

4 Place the cornflour in a cup or small bowl and mix with a couple of tablespoons of cold water until smooth. Take the dish out of the oven and stir in the cornflour then return to the oven, uncovered this time, to cook for a further half an hour. This will let the cornflour cook through and thicken the sauce. Remove the dish from the oven and season to taste.

Cook's notes Allergy suitability: dairy/gluten/wheat/yeast free (depending on the content of the stock) • Medium GL • Can be made in advance • Suitable for freezing

Lamb Burgers with Avocado and Mixed Bean and Tomato Salad

These Greek-style lamb burgers make a change to beef. As lamb is a fattier meat, they are best cooked under the grill to drain away the excess fat. Alternatively, you could barbecue them over a moderate heat if you prefer – just try to avoid charring them. Serve the burgers and bean salad either on their own or with a green salad and wholemeal pitta, with slices of Pine Nut and Roasted Pepper Corn Bread on page 144, or quinoa.

SERVES 4 (one large or two small burgers each)

Burgers
600g (1lb 5½oz) minced lamb
3 tbsp finely chopped, flat-leaf parsley
2 heaped tsp dried oregano
1 heaped tsp ground cumin
1 heaped tsp ground coriander
1 heaped tsp sea salt
Lots of freshly ground black pepper

Mixed bean and tomato salad
1 tbsp mild olive oil
1 garlic clove, crushed
1 red onion, diced
125g (4½oz) cherry tomatoes, halved
4 heaped tbsp tomato passata
Splash of red wine (optional)
125g (4½oz) pitted and drained Kalamata olives, halved
410g can mixed pulses, rinsed and drained
2 tsp balsamic vinegar, or to taste
1 dessertspoon dried oregano, or to taste
Freshly ground black pepper

To serve
2 ripe avocados

1 First prepare the burgers. Mix the minced lamb with the herbs and seasonings, and shape into four large or eight small, evenly sized patties. Flatten with your hand, place on a plate and chill in the fridge. Preheat the grill to a medium heat.

2 Meanwhile, make the mixed bean and tomato salad. Heat the oil in a large frying pan or saucepan and sweat the garlic and onion for three to five minutes, to soften. Add the tomatoes and simmer for another five minutes or so, until they soften and start to disintegrate.

3 Add the tomato passata, red wine if using, olives, mixed pulses, balsamic and oregano and simmer to thicken the sauce. Now add the black pepper, stir and taste to check the flavour. Cover and set to one side while you cook the burgers.

4 Grill the burgers for around five minutes each side (for larger burgers; smaller ones will take a little less) or until the burgers are cooked through (if you are pregnant, check to make sure that the juices run clear and that the flesh in the middle is not pink). Serve with thinly sliced avocado (if necessary, squeezed with lemon juice to prevent discolouration) and any other accompaniments.

Cook's notes Allergy suitability: gluten/wheat/dairy free • Can be made in advance

Fish

Fish is pretty quick to cook, making it a great fast food choice when time is tight or when you are tired. Fish is also an excellent source of protein and valuable minerals like zinc, which plays a vital role in conception and pregnancy. Oily fish, like salmon, trout, mackerel, herrings, kippers, sardines and anchovies also contain the beneficial omega-3 essential fats that are so important for our health and for that of a developing baby. Fresh (not canned) tuna does also contain some omega-3 fats but in lesser amounts. Plus, carnivorous fish like tuna, shark, marlin and swordfish should be avoided during pregnancy in order to avoid contamination with mercury, a toxic heavy metal from polluted waters, which accumulates in larger, carnivorous fish. Standard advice during pregnancy is not to eat more than two portions of oily fish like trout, mackerel, herrings, kippers, sardines and tuna per week to limit any exposure to such pollutants, although salmon and anchovies do not tend to be high in mercury and so they are a safer bet.

The following selection of recipes includes a range of flavours and cooking methods, from the Eastern inspired Thai-style Fish Balls on page 119 and Fish, Cauliflower and Chickpea Curry on page 122 to the distinctly British Easy Fish Pie on page 124 and Cheat's Fish Cakes on page 125.

If you are put off by the thought of fish, particularly during pregnancy when taste buds tend to be fickle at the best of times, be reassured by the fact that many of these dishes feature fish in an easy to eat manner, for example, being concealed in fish balls, fish pie and fish cakes. Equally, if you are already a fish fan, I hope that the recipes offer some interesting and varied ideas to expand your usual repertoire, such as using mackerel in a Niçoise salad and making Thai-style Fish Balls as an alternative to the standard fish cake.

Sesame Salmon with a Chilli and Spring Onion Quinoa Salad

This very simple salmon dish will help you to effortlessly increase your intake of good omega-3 fats. The fresh, Asian flavours of this sesame-coated salmon and quinoa salad are ideal in hot weather or if you don't feel like heavy, stodgy food. Plus, did you know that quinoa contains more calcium than milk? Calcium is essential during pregnancy for both mother and baby, and quinoa is a great source for anyone who is worried about their levels or who avoids dairy products. The chickpeas also provide phyto-oestrogens, which help to keep hormone levels in balance, for anyone trying to conceive. Steamed pak choi is a good accompaniment.

SERVES 2

Quinoa salad

100g (4oz) quinoa

1/2 tsp sea salt

410g can chickpeas, rinsed and drained

1 tbsp toasted sesame oil, or to taste

1 tbsp tamari (wheat-free soy sauce) or soy sauce, or to taste

1 tbsp rice vinegar

1 tbsp fresh lemon juice

8 spring onions, finely sliced

2 tsp finely chopped mild red chilli, deseeded

1 tbsp finely chopped coriander or flat-leaf parsley or spinach leaves

Freshly ground black pepper

Sesame salmon

2 salmon fillets

A little mild olive oil

Sea salt

2 tbsp sesame seeds, for coating

A little extra tamari (wheat-free soy sauce) or soy sauce

Toasted sesame oil and lemon juice for drizzling

1 Cook the quinoa with the salt according to the pack instructions (as a rule of thumb, cover with just over two parts water to one part quinoa, cover and simmer for around 10 minutes then leave to sit, covered, for a further five minutes to let the grains soak up all the water and fluff up).

2 Add the remaining salad ingredients and stir then adjust the seasoning to taste. Set to one side.

3 Next cook the salmon. Rub the fillets all over with a little oil and salt then press the seeds onto the flesh side. If you are using a non-stick frying pan, add a tablespoon or so of oil to a frying pan big enough to easily accommodate both salmon fillets (they should not be touching). Get the pan hot and fry the salmon for around six to seven minutes per side until golden and cooked through (the flesh should flake easily when pressed). Take care not to let the seeds get too dark and burn on top.

4 Plate up the salad and place the salmon on top. Drizzle the fish with a dash of tamari or soy, toasted sesame oil and lemon juice, to taste, and serve immediately.

Cook's notes Allergy suitability: gluten/wheat/dairy free (use gluten-free tamari if necessary) • Can be made in advance (quinoa only)

Spiced Salmon, Tenderstem Broccoli and Soba Noodle Stir-fry

Tenderstem broccoli is far richer in antioxidants than standard broccoli, but either would work well, or use purple sprouting broccoli during its short summer growing season. The stir-fry ingredients make good use of strong-flavoured Thai ingredients like chilli and coriander, which prime your digestive system to cope with the meal ahead. Shiitake mushrooms – a symbol of longevity in Asia – contain lentinan, a polysaccharide known to support the immune system, as well as having a particularly high amino acid, vitamin and mineral content. They have a have woody, smoky flavour but you can use any mushroom if they are unavailable.

SERVES 4

175g (6oz) soba noodles

200g (7oz) tenderstem broccoli

1 tbsp mild oil

125g (4½oz) shiitake mushrooms

2 x salmon fillets, skinned and cubed (275g/10oz)

200g (7oz) bok choi or spring greens

400ml can coconut milk

A handful or bunch of coriander

Spice blend

1 mild red chilli, deseeded

1 large garlic clove

1 tsp grated fresh root ginger

2 tsp vegetable bouillon powder

Zest and juice of a lime

10 spring onions

2 tbsp fish sauce or tamari (wheat-free soy sauce)

1 tbsp toasted sesame oil

1 Cook the noodles according to the pack instructions then refresh by plunging into cold water (this helps them not to stick together). Steam the broccoli until al dente, refresh then cut into short pieces.

2 Heat the oil in a wok or large frying pan. Add the mushrooms, stir-fry for a couple of minutes then add the broccoli. Cover the vegetables in the pan with a couple of pieces of kitchen towel soaked in cold water to allow them to steam-fry for around four minutes, so that the broccoli starts to soften but still remains bright green.

3 Meanwhile, whiz up the spice blend in a food processor.

4 Add the cubed fish, bok choi or greens, coconut milk and blended spice mixture to the wok or pan. Stir, cover and simmer for around five minutes to allow the fish and broccoli to cook through.

5 Finally, stir in the noodles and coriander and serve immediately.

Cook's notes Allergy suitability: gluten/wheat/dairy/yeast free (if necessary, check that the soba noodles are 100 per cent buckwheat, which is gluten free, as some brands contain wheat)

Thai-style Fish Balls

This light, Asian-inspired fish dish is brimming with flavour as well as with digestion-helping herbs like coriander. Plus, of course, making this with oily fish like salmon will provide omega-3 fats. If you are skinning the fish fillets yourself try to shave off as much flesh next to the skin as possible (this may well be brown or grey), as this is where the omega-3 essential fats are found. You could also use firm-fleshed white fish like haddock. Serve with stir-fried vegetables and brown rice or noodles.

SERVES 2

2 skinned and boned salmon fillets (300g/11oz)

1 garlic clove, crushed

1 tbsp peeled, roughly chopped fresh root ginger

4 spring onions, topped and tailed

1 lemongrass stalk, tough outer layers removed

2 tbsp fresh coriander leaves and stems

1 tbsp nam pla (Thai fish sauce)

1 tbsp toasted sesame oil

25g (1oz) sesame seeds (optional)

1 Preheat the oven to 180°C/350°F/gas mark 4.

2 Put the fish, garlic, ginger, spring onions, lemongrass, coriander, nam pla and sesame oil into a food processor and blend until the mixture is very finely chopped and well combined. Alternatively, if you do not have a blender you could finely chop the ingredients by hand and mix together. This will give a coarser texture.

3 Shape into six small balls then roll in the sesame seeds to coat, if using. Place the balls on a lightly greased or lined baking tray and cook for around 15 minutes or until the fish is cooked through (the fish should look white the whole way through).

Cook's notes Allergy suitability: gluten/wheat/dairy/yeast free • Can be prepared in advance • Suitable for freezing

Simple Trout Parcels

This dish is absolutely delicious. You will love it. At the first testing session I had to wrestle the plate back off my husband Nick. It's so simple yet so full of fresh, Oriental flavours and, of course, very rich in protein and essential fats from the fish to nourish you before and during pregnancy. Serve on a bed of steamed spinach with brown basmati rice or noodles.

SERVES 2

2 tbsp tamari (wheat-free soy sauce) or soy sauce

1 tsp xylitol (or caster sugar)

1/2 a mild red chilli, deseeded and very finely chopped

1 tbsp rice vinegar

2.5cm (1in) chunk root ginger, peeled and grated or finely chopped

3 spring onions, very finely sliced

2 trout fillets (salmon would also work)

1 Preheat the grill to very hot.

2 Stir the tamari or soy sauce, xylitol or sugar, chilli, rice vinegar, ginger and spring onions together.

3 Spread out a large piece of kitchen foil on a baking sheet and lay the fillets in the middle (not touching, in order to allow the heat to circulate and cook them more quickly). Pour the sauce over the top of each fillet.

4 Fold the foil to seal the fish and sauce inside the parcel.

5 Cook for around eight to 10 minutes, or a little longer, depending on the heat of your grill – carefully open the parcel to check if the flesh if firm when pressed and flakes easily. Take care as the steam will be very hot. You can always reseal the parcel and return to the heat for a few more minutes.

Cook's notes Allergy suitability: gluten, wheat, dairy free (choose a gluten-free tamari if necessary) • Can be prepared in advance (chill until ready to cook)

Fish, Cauliflower and Chickpea Curry

This is a light, fibre-rich curry that will top up your energy levels thanks to the coconut milk. Coconut milk is a rich source of special saturated fatty acid, lauric acid, that is readily used as fuel rather than being stored as fat. Choose a firm-fleshed fish fillet such as haddock loin. The chickpeas provide phyto-oestrogens; compounds which appear to help balance hormone levels. The spinach contributes two crucial pregnancy minerals; iron and folic acid. Serve with brown basmati rice.

SERVES 2

1 tbsp coconut oil or mild olive oil

1 red onion, sliced

1/2 mild red chilli, deseeded and finely chopped

1 tbsp mild or medium curry powder or Madras spice blend

110ml (31/2fl oz) hot vegetable stock

400ml can coconut milk

410g can chickpeas, rinsed and drained

1/2 a cauliflower, cut into small florets

275g (10oz) skinned and boned firm-fleshed fish fillet, such as haddock

100g (4oz) baby leaf spinach, chopped

2 tbsp flat-leaf parsley, finely chopped

1 tsp sea salt

Juice of a lemon

1 Heat the oil in a large pan, add the onion and and sweat it for three to four minutes to soften. Add the chilli and curry powder and cook for a further minute.

2 Stir in the stock and coconut milk, chickpeas and small cauliflower florets (if they are too big they will not cook in the simmering time), cover and simmer for around 15–20 minutes to soften the cauliflower.

3 Cut the fish into evenly sized chunks, add to the pan and simmer for a minute then add the spinach and stir gently to let it wilt and allow the fish to finish cooking (it should take around three to five minutes in total and will flake easily when cooked).

4 Stir in the parsley and salt and taste to check the flavour. Serve in bowls and squeeze fresh lemon juice over the top, to taste (this cuts through the creamy coconut milk and heat from the chilli).

Cook's notes Allergy suitability: gluten/wheat/dairy/yeast free (depending on the stock content)

Quick Kedgeree

It is a little bit of a stretch, in fact, to call this recipe kedgeree as it uses mackerel rather than haddock. There are two good reasons for this however: firstly, mackerel is an oily fish, providing essential omega-3 fats to nourish your baby and protect your own health and, secondly, smoked mackerel does not require pre-cooking, making the recipe much quicker and easier to make. This is a complete meal to provide long-lasting energy and plentiful nutrients. You could also add a couple of hard-boiled eggs, peeled and quartered, to make it more like a traditional kedgeree, if wished.

SERVES 2

150g (5oz) smoked mackerel fillets
100g (4oz) brown basmati rice
75g (3oz) frozen peas
1 tbsp chopped flat-leaf parsley leaves
Good squeeze of lemon juice, to taste
Freshly ground black pepper

1 Skin and flake the mackerel into bite-sized pieces, checking for bones as you do so.

2 Cook the rice according to the pack instructions. Add the peas for the last three minutes to cook through before you drain the rice.

3 Stir the flaked fish and parsley into the rice. Season to taste with lemon juice and black pepper – and a little salt if needs be, but the fish should provide adequate saltiness.

Cook's notes Allergy suitability: gluten/wheat/dairy free • Medium GL • Can be prepared in advance

Easy Fish Pie

If like me you crave old-fashioned nursery food or stodge during your pregnancy, this fish pie fits the bill without being overly heavy. The texture is just right, with flakes of firm-fleshed fish covered in a creamy white sauce and topped with smooth mashed potato. There are countless ways to make a fish pie, but I have pared this dish back to basics, to make it as easy and quick as possible to throw together. Serve with peas and carrots.

SERVES 3–4

200g (7oz) skinless, firm-fleshed white fish fillet such as pollack

200g (7oz) skinless, undyed smoked haddock fillet

300ml (1/2pt) semi-skimmed milk

Small bunch flat-leaf parsley, finely chopped (optional)

500g (1lb 2oz) unpeeled floury potatoes, cut into chunks

50g (2oz) slightly salted butter

25g (1oz) plain flour

Sea salt

Freshly ground black pepper

1 Place the fillets in a frying pan big enough to accommodate them all in a single layer then pour the milk over. Heat so that the milk starts to bubble then reduce the heat and simmer gently for eight minutes or until the fish flakes easily when pressed. Carefully remove the fish from the pan, place on a plate and flake into large pieces. Place the pieces in a medium pie dish (around 18cm/7in) and scatter the parsley over the top. Pour the cooking milk into a jug and reserve.

2 Preheat the oven to 200°C/400°F/gas mark 6. Place the potato chunks in a pan and cover with cold water. Bring to the boil, cover and cook for around 20 minutes to soften. Meanwhile, make the sauce.

3 Melt the butter in a pan then stir in the flour and cook for a minute, stirring constantly to keep it smooth. Reduce the heat and stir in a splash of the poaching milk, gradually adding more and more as you stir, to form a smooth, thick sauce – but leave around 100ml (3fl oz) or a small cupful of milk for the mashed potato. Season with salt and pepper to taste (don't add too much salt as the smoked haddock will also help to season the dish) then pour over the fish.

4 When the potatoes are cooked, drain and mash with the remaining milk to form a smooth mash. Season with salt to taste. Place the mash on top of the fish and sauce, covering the entire dish right to the edges, and fluff up the top with a fork. Bake in the preheated oven for 30 minutes.

Cook's notes Medium GL • Suitable for freezing • Can be made in advance (make the day before, chill and cook for an extra 10 minutes)

Cheat's Fish Cakes

So-called because I have purposefully used a standard pack of smoked mackerel in this recipe to remove the need for cooking the fish before you make the fish cakes. This is a very simple dish to make and to eat – it's real comfort food which also provides valuable omega-3 essential fats for your baby's brain and eye development and your own hormonal and skin health. Good with peas and/or carrots.

SERVES 4 (you can freeze any leftovers or chill them for the next day)

500g (1lb 2oz) unpeeled floury potatoes, chopped

Knob or two of butter (or dairy-free margarine)

300g (11oz) smoked mackerel

Good squeeze of lemon juice

1 handful fresh flat-leaf parsley, chopped

Freshly ground black pepper

1 free-range or organic egg, beaten

1 tbsp plain flour or cornflour

1 Boil the potatoes for around 20 minutes to soften, then drain and mash with the butter until smooth.

2 Flake the fish and add to the potato, mashing well with a fork to break up any fish chunks.

3 Stir in the lemon juice, parsley and plenty of black pepper. Taste the mixture and adjust the seasoning if necessary. You shouldn't need any added salt as the smoked fish provides plenty of flavour. Mix the egg into the mixture to help it stick together (apologies for stating the obvious but if you are pregnant don't taste again after this stage due to the raw egg).

4 Preheat the grill to medium hot. Shape the mixture into fish cakes. Sprinkle the flour on a plate then dust the fish cakes with flour on both sides.

5 Grill on kitchen foil under the preheated grill for around 12 minutes per side, or until golden and firm on top.

Cook's notes Allergy suitability: gluten/wheat/dairy free (if using cornflour and dairy-free margarine) • Medium GL • Can be made in advance • Suitable for freezing

Mackerel Niçoise

Niçoise normally features tuna fish of course, but mackerel is not only a better source of omega-3 essential fats, it is also less contaminated with heavy metals like mercury. I've specified Cos or Romaine lettuce but you can use your favourite. This filling salad makes a delicious main meal that is packed with fibre-rich vegetables plus plenty of protein. The portions are very generous so you shouldn't need any accompaniments.

SERVES 2 (very generously!)

2 free-range or organic eggs

200g (7oz) fine green beans, topped and tailed

Romaine or Cos lettuce, washed and torn into bite-sized pieces

2 tomatoes, cut into wedges

410g can mixed pulses, rinsed and drained

100g (4oz) black olives, halved or roughly chopped

6 small anchovy fillets, quartered or roughly chopped

1 tbsp capers, rinsed (optional)

Juice of a lemon, or to taste

6 tbsp extra virgin olive oil

Freshly ground black pepper and sea salt, to taste

250g jar mackerel fillets in olive oil, drained

1 Hard boil the eggs for around eight minutes then cool in cold water before peeling and quartering.

2 Boil or steam the green beans for around five minutes in salted water, until al dente, then drain and reserve.

3 Toss the lettuce, tomatoes, pulses, olives and anchovies (and capers if using) in a large bowl with the cooked beans.

4 Add the lemon juice and oil and toss to coat then season to taste. Finally, gently fold in the egg and mackerel fillets to avoid breaking them up too much.

Cook's notes Allergy suitability: gluten/wheat/dairy free • Can be made in advance (although best served fresh, and add the fish just before serving)

Vegetarian

Unlike many vegetarian recipes and meat-free meals on menus or in supermarkets, the meals in this section have been designed to provide complete protein. By this I mean that they provide the amino acids essential to health that must be obtained from our diet. Animal foods like meat, fish, eggs and dairy products provide these amino acids naturally, but plant-based foods often need a little more consideration. Nuts, seeds, quinoa (in fact the seed of a fruit) and soya beans are good sources of protein, but other beans and pulses such as lentils, chickpeas and kidney beans fall short, as do grains. Eating these foods together, however, tops up any individual shortfalls to give you a more balanced dish.

Sufficient protein is important to enable your body to repair and rebuild, to help keep blood sugar balanced, to produce the neurotransmitters which allow your brain to process information and, lastly, to help the liver detoxify waste. Protein is also, of course, crucial for the growth and development of your baby and as such vegetarians and vegans in particular should pay attention to their protein intake during pregnancy.

The good news is that this section makes it easy to meet your protein needs. I have also made use of an array of different protein-rich ingredients to offer variety and interest as well as better nutritional balance. This is important as it is all too easy for vegetarians to get stuck in a rut, relying on dairy foods or processed meat substitutes for their protein requirements. While there is nothing wrong with cheese, dairy foods can be hard to digest and are a common cause of allergies. They can also cause inflammation in the body, so they may make symptoms of inflammatory conditions such as hay fever, asthma and eczema worse. Processed meat substitutes are very often heavily laced with additives and flavourings, and as such are best avoided or certainly eaten in moderation only.

For anyone who is worried about their calcium consumption, particularly during pregnancy when your requirements increase, nuts and seeds and dark green leafy vegetables – all foods that are used liberally in this cookbook – are also good sources of this bone-building mineral. Plus, the carefully chosen dairy products used in some of the recipes in this book, such as the live natural yoghurt with breakfast and the delicious Grilled Goat's Cheese with Warm Puy Lentil Salad on page 132, will help to top up your levels.

Spiced Cashew and Carrot Burgers

This recipe is a great way to top up your levels of skin-supporting vitamin E and beta-carotene, thanks to the sweet potato and carrot. Both of these antioxidant nutrients are helpful in avoiding stretch marks and maintaining a healthy immune system. These burgers are absolutely delicious and are packed with fibre and vegetarian protein. They can be served in wholemeal pitta breads and/or with salad.

SERVES 2

100g (4oz) split red lentils

1 medium (135g/5oz) sweet potato, unpeeled and diced

1 tbsp coconut or mild olive oil

1 garlic clove, crushed

1 red onion, diced

1 celery stick, finely sliced

1 medium carrot, finely sliced

50g (2oz) cashew nuts (or sunflower seeds if you are avoiding nuts)

1 tsp ground cumin

1 tsp ground coriander

1 tsp sea salt

Freshly ground black pepper

1 medium free-range or organic egg

1 Place the lentils and diced sweet potato in a saucepan and just cover with water. Simmer, covered, for around 15 minutes until just soft (do not allow them to get mushy – you want them to hold their shape as much as possible).

2 Preheat the oven to 200°C/400°F/gas mark 6. Line a baking tray with non-stick baking paper.

3 Heat the oil in a small frying pan, add the garlic, onion, celery and carrot and sweat for around five minutes to soften.

4 Place in a food processor along with the lentils and sweet potato, cashew nuts, cumin and coriander. Blend until fairly smooth and combined. Season to taste, mix in the beaten egg and shape into patties. Place on the baking tray and cook for around 40 minutes or until slightly coloured on top and firm to the touch.

Cook's notes Allergy suitability: gluten/wheat/dairy/yeast free • Medium GL • Vegetarian • Can be made in advance • Suitable for freezing

Fried Rice with Oriental Mushrooms and Cashew Nuts

This delicious, one-pot mixture is extremely quick and easy to make and is not only far more nutritious than fried rice from a takeaway, but I think it also tastes better. Using brown basmati rice makes this dish far richer in fibre, vitamins and minerals, as well as being more filling and less fattening than the standard version featuring white rice. You can also vary the dish to use up any leftovers, and meat eaters could add chopped meat, flaked fish or prawns. Look out for packs of exotic mixed mushrooms in supermarkets or find them in Chinese supermarkets, otherwise use a mixture of shiitake and ordinary mushrooms, or just ordinary mushrooms.

SERVES 2

150g (5oz) brown basmati rice (or 'low-GL' rice)

2 tbsp coconut, sesame or mild olive oil

2 heaped tbsp unsalted cashew nuts

250g (9oz) exotic mixed mushrooms such as shiitake and oyster, sliced or torn

2 garlic cloves, finely sliced

2 bunches of spring onions, finely sliced

2 free-range or organic eggs, beaten

2 tbsp tamari (wheat-free soy sauce) or soy sauce

1 tbsp toasted sesame oil

Handful of roughly chopped coriander leaves (optional)

1 Cook the rice following the instructions on the packet but do not add salt to the pan or it will be too salty once the tamari or soy is added. Drain and cool.

2 Heat a tablespoon of the oil in a large wok or frying pan, add the cashew nuts and stir-fry for a minute or two until golden (these will burn very easily so take care). Remove from the pan and reserve.

3 Add the mushrooms and garlic to the pan and stir-fry for around five to eight minutes or until the mushrooms soften and shrink. Add the spring onions and stir-fry for another minute or so. Add another tablespoon of oil to the pan at this stage to stop everything sticking to the bottom.

4 Pour in the eggs and stir-fry for 30 seconds to scramble quickly then add the cooked rice. Stir for a minute or so then add the tamari or soy and sesame oil and the cashew nuts. Scatter the coriander over the top and serve immediately.

Cook's notes Allergy suitability: gluten/wheat/dairy free (use gluten-free tamari if necessary) • Medium GL • Vegetarian

Barley Risotto

This recipe is endlessly variable according to what you have to hand or, during pregnancy, to what your fickle taste buds permit you to eat. For flavourings, try one of the suggestions below or you can use up leftovers like cooked chicken or ham, or flaked salmon, and vegetables such as mushrooms or asparagus. Barley is a good source of fibre and niacin (vitamin B_3), as well as calcium, magnesium and potassium – all crucial in pregnancy. Choose pot barley if you can find it as unlike pearl barley this is the whole grain. Soak the pot barley for at least six hours or overnight. If you can't get pot barley, pearl barely works just as well and doesn't need to be soaked. Parmesan and pecorino are unpasturised but in fact both cheeses are too hard for the Listeria bacteria to grow.

SERVES 4 (can be reheated for an easy meal the next day)

Basic risotto
2 tbsp mild olive oil

2 garlic cloves, crushed

I red onion, diced

300g (11oz) pot or pearly barley (if using pot barley, soak it for at least six hours)

1.25L (2pt) hot vegetable stock

A little sea salt, to taste (optional)

Freshly ground black pepper

Sweet potato and sage risotto
I unpeeled sweet potato, diced

I tbsp mild olive oil

I tsp dried sage

Parmesan

Flaked almonds (optional)

Pea and spinach risotto
125g (4½oz) peas

125g (4½oz) baby leaf spinach

Lemon juice, to taste

Pecorino or Parmesan

I First make the risotto base. Heat the oil in a large saucepan, add the garlic and onion and sweat for around three minutes to start to soften. Tip the barley into the pan and stir.

2 Add the stock, stir, bring to the boil then cover and reduce the heat to simmer for around an hour, stirring occasionally, until the grains are soft and the stock has almost all been absorbed. Season to taste.

To make the sweet potato risotto, first heat the oven to 200°C/400°F/gas mark 6. Toss the diced sweet potato in the oil then roast it for around 30 minutes until soft, turning halfway through. About 10 minutes before the basic risotto is cooked, toss the sweet potato and sage through the risotto, to help the soft sweet potato almost melt into the mixture. Add a handful of Parmesan shavings or toasted, flaked almonds (or both) per person just before serving.

To make the pea and spinach risotto, cook the peas and wilt the spinach then stir into the risotto base. Add a squeeze of lemon juice and/or some Pecorino (a hard sheep's cheese) or Parmesan shavings for extra flavour.

Cook's notes Allergy suitability: wheat/dairy free • Vegetarian • Medium GL • Can be made in advance (reheat until piping hot)

Grilled Goat's Cheese with a Warm Puy Lentil Salad

A delicious and very easy mix that is equally successful served as a starter – in which case serve a half portion per person. Lentils are rich in folic acid, which is of course crucial in pregnancy. Puy lentils hold their shape well when cooked but you could equally use ordinary green lentils. Goat's cheese can be eaten when pregnant as long as it is heated through. Goat's and sheep's milk products tend to be easier to digest than cow's milk versions, making them a better choice for cheese lovers and those people with a dairy intolerance.

SERVES 2

150g (5oz) dried Puy lentils

2 tsp vegetable bouillon powder

1 red onion, diced

1 tbsp mild olive oil

Handful of flat-leaf parsley, chopped

1–2 tbsp extra virgin olive oil (I like to use the oil from the sun-blush tomatoes)

2 x 100g (4oz) goat's cheese rounds with rind, cut into 2 if necessary

2 tbsp walnut halves, roughly chopped

Freshly ground black pepper

2 heaped tbsp roughly chopped sun-blush tomatoes

Sea salt, to taste, as required

1 Cover the lentils with two parts boiling water to one part lentils and add the bouillon powder. Bring to boil then cover and simmer until just tender (around 20 minutes). Drain off any excess water.

2 Fry the diced red onion in the olive oil until soft and translucent then mix into the lentils and season to taste. Add the parsley and extra virgin olive oil to give it a lovely gloss. Keep the lentil mixture warm.

3 Preheat the grill then grill the goat's cheese for around five minutes or until golden and bubbling on top.

4 Meanwhile, lightly toast the walnuts in a dry frying pan.

5 Place a warm mound of lentil mixture in middle of each plate, top with the goat's cheese then scatter the walnut halves and black pepper over the top. Finish the dish by sprinkling the the sun-blush tomato pieces around the mound of lentils.

Cook's notes Allergy suitability: gluten/wheat free • Vegetarian • Can be made in advance (the lentil mixture)

Puy Lentils with Porcini Mushrooms and Thyme

This unusual vegetarian dish combines delicious flavours and textures from the Puy lentils, which retain their bite upon cooking, to the meaty, smoky porcini mushrooms and the aromatic scent of thyme. The lentils and walnuts (these can be replaced with pumpkin seeds if you are avoiding nuts) provide protein and the fibre content of this dish is also very high.

SERVES 2

25g (1oz) dried porcini mushrooms

200g (7oz) dried Puy lentils or 400g can cooked lentils

1 tbsp mild olive oil

2 garlic cloves, crushed

1 red onion, diced

1 celery stick, finely chopped

2 leeks, finely chopped

50g (2oz) walnut pieces, roughly chopped (or pumpkin seeds if avoiding nuts)

1 tbsp fresh thyme sprigs, or to taste

1 tsp sea salt

Freshly ground black pepper

1 Soak the porcini for 30 minutes in warm water then drain, reserving the liquor to cook the lentils. Cook the lentils according to the pack instructions if using dried – include the liquor from the soaked mushrooms to add flavour.

2 Meanwhile, heat the oil in a small frying pan and sauté the garlic, onion, celery and leeks for a couple of minutes then cover and sweat for a further five minutes to soften.

3 Add the lentils, soaked mushrooms and walnuts (or pumpkin seeds) to the pan of sautéed vegetables and stir in. Add the thyme and seasoning.

Cook's notes Allergy suitability: gluten/wheat/dairy/yeast free • Medium GL • Vegetarian • Can be made in advance

Wild Rice Salad with Rosemary Roasted Vegetables

Wild rice is not in fact a grain at all but a grass and is much richer in protein and minerals than rice itself. It takes longer to cook, so soaking it beforehand reduces the cooking time enormously. This dairy-free dish is delicious and filling served simply with a mixed leaf salad but can also be served with grilled goat's cheese, griddled halloumi or crumbled feta cheese (which is safe to eat during pregnancy). This recipe makes a lot, but it's the sort of thing people go back to for second helpings, or leftovers make a wonderfully easy lunch the next day – store in the fridge.

SERVES 6

250g (9oz) wild rice

150g (5oz) dried Puy lentils

2 courgettes, cut into bite-sized chunks

2 red onions, cut into wedges

2 red, yellow or orange peppers, cut into bite-sized chunks

4 whole garlic cloves

2 tbsp mild olive oil

2 sprigs of rosemary

1 tsp vegetable bouillon powder

100g (4oz) pitted Kalamata olives, roughly chopped

20 pieces sun-blush tomato, roughly chopped

2 tbsp marinating oil from the sun-blush tomatoes

Good handful basil leaves, torn or chopped

Juice of a lemon

Freshly ground black pepper

A little sea salt

1 Place the wild rice and lentils in a large saucepan and pour over boiling water. Cover and soak for four hours to soften and reduce the cooking time.

2 Preheat the oven to 180°C/350°F/gas mark 4. Place the courgettes, onions, peppers and garlic in a roasting tin, drizzle with the oil from the jar of tomatoes (or mild olive oil), stir to coat evenly then place the rosemary on top. Place in the oven for around 45 minutes to an hour, taking the tray out and stirring halfway through to turn all the vegetables.

3 Half an hour into the vegetables' cooking time, drain the soaked rice and lentils, return them to the saucepan with the vegetable bouillon and re-cover with 600ml (1pt) boiling water. Bring to the boil then cover and simmer for about 20 minutes or until cooked and the water has been absorbed.

4 When the vegetables are cooked (they should be soft when pierced), remove the stalks from the rosemary and discard. Fold the vegetables into the cooked rice and lentils and stir in the remaining ingredients. Taste and adjust the seasoning if needed.

Cook's notes Allergy suitability: gluten/wheat/dairy free • Medium GL • Vegetarian • Can be made in advance

Baked Sweet Potato with Hummus

Doubtless you don't need me to tell you how to bake a potato, but I have included the recipe here as it is such a simple meal to prepare but one which is surprisingly filling and nutritious. Sweet potatoes are a better choice than standard potatoes as their bright orange flesh shows how rich they are in the antioxidant vitamin beta-carotene. This is converted by the body into vitamin A – a vital nutrient to nourish a pregnancy, but one which can be dangerous in excess during pregnancy. As the body will regulate how much vitamin A it converts from beta-carotene, beta-carotene-rich foods like sweet potatoes are a safe way to top up your levels. Plus, sweet potatoes are rich in vitamin E to keep skin soft and supple and less prone to stretch marks. They also help the body to keep blood sugar levels in balance, despite their high starch content. For the hummus you can either follow this standard recipe or try the Pine Nut and Sun-dried Pepper version on page 97. Or, to save time, buy a pot from the deli.

SERVES 2

2 medium sweet potatoes

410g can chickpeas in water, rinsed and drained

Juice of ½ a lemon, or to taste

1 large garlic clove, crushed

1 tbsp tahini, or to taste

75ml (2½fl oz) extra virgin olive oil

1 tsp sea salt, or to taste

1 Preheat the oven to 200°C/400°F/gas mark 6. Cut a slit in the middle of each sweet potato then place on a baking sheet and cook for around 45 minutes to an hour or until soft when pressed.

2 To make the hummus, blend all of the remaining ingredients until smooth and creamy. Adjust the seasoning to taste, and add more oil or a splash of water to loosen the consistency, if preferred.

3 Split the cooked sweet potato open and add a dollop of hummus. Serve with a side salad.

Cook's notes Allergy suitability: gluten/wheat/dairy/yeast free • Vegetarian • Medium GL • The hummus can be made in advance

Quinoa Salad with Olives, Tomatoes and Pine Nuts

This delicious dish is very quick and easy to make and provides plenty of protein, calcium and zinc – all essential nutrients before and after conception. It does not need any added salt as the olives and feta provide enough flavour. Quinoa is a source of complete protein for vegetarians, so there is no nutritional need to add the feta unless, like me, you want to! This salad is good with the Griddled Peppers and Courgettes on page 151, or a green salad.

SERVES 4

300g (11oz) quinoa, rinsed and drained

1 tsp salt

75g (3oz) pitted Kalamata olives, roughly chopped

100g (4oz) pine nuts or roughly chopped walnut halves (or pumpkin seeds if avoiding nuts)

125g (4¹/₂oz) sun-blush tomatoes in olive oil, roughly chopped

100g (4oz) young spinach leaves, finely chopped

A handful of basil leaves, finely chopped

Juice of ¹/₂ a lemon, or to taste

100g (4oz) feta, crumbled (optional)

Freshly ground black pepper

1 Cook the quinoa with the salt according to the pack instructions (as a rule of thumb, cover with just over two parts water to one part quinoa, cover and simmer for around 10 minutes then leave to sit, covered, for a further five minutes to let the grains soak up all the water and fluff up).

2 Stir in the olives, nuts (or pumpkin seeds), tomatoes and a couple of tablespoons of the marinating oil, spinach, basil and lemon juice.

3 Fold in the feta if using and season to taste with black pepper.

Cook's notes Allergy suitability: gluten/wheat/yeast free/dairy/ (if omitting feta) • Vegetarian • Can be made in advance

Chickpea and Spinach Curry

This is an incredibly quick and easy recipe for when time or energy are in short supply. It contains plenty of fibre to make it filling and easy to digest, plus iron and folic acid from the spinach. Don't be put off by the saturated fat content of the coconut milk – this kind of plant-based fat contains appears to be readily used for energy rather than being stored as fat. You could omit the fresh chilli for a milder flavour. Serve with brown basmati (or 'low-GL') rice. A salad of diced cucumber, tomatoes and red onion also makes a nice accompaniment.

SERVES 2

1 tbsp coconut or mild olive oil

1 red onion, sliced

1/2 mild red chilli, deseeded and finely chopped

1 tbsp mild or medium curry powder or Madras spice blend

75ml (21/2fl oz) hot vegetable stock

250ml (8fl oz) coconut milk

410g can chickpeas, rinsed and drained

1 tsp sea salt, or to taste

100g (4oz) baby leaf spinach, chopped

1 Heat the oil in a large pan, add the onion and sweat for three to four minutes to soften. Add the chilli and curry powder and cook for a further minute.

2 Stir in the stock, coconut milk and chickpeas and simmer for 15 minutes to reduce the sauce and allow the flavours to combine. Season with salt and taste to check the flavour.

3 A couple of minutes before you want to serve, stir in the spinach and let it warm through.

Cook's notes Allergy suitability: gluten/wheat/dairy/yeast free (depending on the stock content) • Vegetarian • Can be made in advance (add the spinach when reheating before serving)

Sweet Potato Frittata

This light dish is easy to make and to eat. The eggs will top up your B vitamin levels – which help to balance hormones before pregnancy, and raise your energy levels and stave off morning sickness during pregnancy. Plus they provide plenty of protein to help a developing baby. Sweet potato (unpeeled for added fibre) is far richer in antioxidant nutrients like vitamin E and beta-carotene than ordinary potatoes. They are also a better bet for maintaining balanced blood sugar levels. This is a complete meal but cheese lovers could throw some grated Cheddar or crumbled feta on top before grilling the frittata, or meat eaters may wish to add some diced (cooked) bacon or ham when pouring in the egg. Serve with the Red Onion, Tomato, Avocado and Basil Salad on page 153 or a simple green salad.

SERVES 4 (any leftovers make an easy meal the next day)

2 tbsp mild olive oil

1 red onion, diced

1 medium sweet potato, unpeeled and diced or finely sliced

6 medium free-range or organic eggs

1 tsp sea salt

Freshly ground black pepper

1 Preheat the grill to medium hot and heat the oil in an ovenproof frying pan over a medium heat. Add the onion and sweet potato and sauté for around 15 minutes until the sweet potato softens.

2 Beat the egg with the salt, pour on top of the vegetables in the pan and cook until the bottom of the omelette is set.

3 Pop under the grill briefly to finish cooking the top of the omelette.

4 Sprinkle with black pepper and slice into wedges.

Cook's notes Allergy suitability: gluten/wheat/dairy/yeast free • Vegetarian

Accompaniments

Never has it been more important that you get your recommended minimum of five portions of fruit and vegetables per day than during pregnancy or while planning a healthy conception. Not only do the vitamins, minerals, antioxidants and other phyto (plant) nutrients help to support health, but the fibre and enzyme content of fresh produce also help your body digest food efficiently and comfortably. Aim to include vegetables in at least two meals per day and favour gentler cooking methods like steaming, stir-frying or steam-frying and slow simmering to minimise the loss of nutrients.

If you struggle to find enthusiasm for vegetables, this section is designed to ignite your appetite for these delicious, nutritious foods. There are plenty of choices here to help you to include a range of different colours and types of vegetables in your diet, as well as interesting and wholesome carbohydrate accompaniments to main meals such as the Herbed Puy Lentils on page 142 and Pine Nut and Roasted Pepper Corn Bread on page 144.

An important rule of thumb to bear in mind is the benefit of consuming a variety of different coloured fruits and vegetables. Try to follow the 'Rainbow Rule', whereby you eat as many different coloured plant foods as possible over a day or week. Each colour denotes a different nutritional value, so you can top up your flavonoid levels when you eat red onions or your beta-carotene levels when you eat yellow or orange foods like squash or sweetcorn, for example.

Herbed Puy Lentils

This is delicious served with grilled fish or meat and the Griddled Peppers and Courgettes on page 151. The quantities and ingredients for this recipe are very relaxed – simply throw in whatever fresh herbs and leaves you have to hand in no particular ratio to create a refreshing, vitamin C-packed salsa verde-style mixture that is perfect stirred through lentils, wild rice or brown rice. Stir in some toasted pine nuts, walnut pieces or pumpkin seeds for extra flavour if wished.

SERVES 4

300g (11oz) dried Puy lentils
1 tsp sea salt
75g (3oz) watercress
150g (5oz) baby leaf spinach
25g (1oz) fresh basil leaves
25g (1oz) flat-leaf parsley leaves
1 large garlic clove, crushed
Juice of 2 lemons
4 tbsp extra virgin olive oil
Freshly ground black pepper
A little extra sea salt, to taste

1 Place the lentils in a large saucepan with the salt and cover with boiling water. Bring to the boil and simmer, covered, for around 20 minutes or until the lentils are cooked (they should be soft and split easily when pressed but will still retain their shape and have a firm texture). Set aside to cool while you make the herby sauce.

2 Blend the leaves and herbs, garlic, lemon juice, oil and black pepper.

3 Stir the mixture into the cooked and cooled lentils and taste to check the flavour – add more lemon, oil or pepper or add some salt if wished.

Cook's notes Allergy suitability: gluten/wheat/dairy/yeast free • Medium GL • Vegetarian • Can be made in advance

Spelt and Seed Bread

Spelt is an ancient grain that has gained celebrity status in recent years due to its high digestibility – unlike its cousin wheat. Many people report that they find spelt far easier to digest, so it is popular with sufferers of irritable bowel syndrome. This simple bread recipe combines whole-grain spelt flour (find it in health food shops or good supermarkets) with seeds to provide protein, minerals and essential fats. Baked in a shallow baking tray, this crumbly, moreish loaf makes an interesting alternative to cornbread or soda bread. It's delicious with a bowl of soup like the Carrot and Lentil Soup on page 90 or with the Pine Nut and Sun-dried Pepper Hummus on page 97.

SERVES 8–12 (freezes well)

200g (7oz) spelt flour

100g (4oz) mixed seeds such as pumpkin, sunflower, sesame, flaxseed, hemp and poppy seeds, roughly ground or chopped

1 tsp sea salt

4 tsp baking powder

225ml (7½fl oz) semi-skimmed milk (or oat or rice milk)

3 medium free-range or organic eggs

5 tbsp mild olive oil

50g (2oz) pumpkin seeds

1 Preheat the oven to 200°C/400°F/gas mark 6. Line a shallow baking tray (around 20 x 30cm/8 x 12in) with baking paper.

2 Place the spelt flour, seed mixture and salt in a mixing bowl and scatter the baking powder on top. Stir to mix thoroughly.

3 Stir the milk, eggs and oil together in a bowl or jug and pour into the dry ingredients, stirring to form a loose dough.

4 Pour into the prepared baking tray, scatter the extra pumpkin seeds evenly over the top and bake for 25 minutes until golden on top and firm to the touch. Cool on a wire rack then cut into squares and store in an airtight container.

Cook's notes Allergy suitability: yeast /dairy free (if using non-dairy milk) • Vegetarian • Can be made in advance • Suitable for freezing

Pine Nut and Roasted Pepper Corn Bread

Corn is a naturally gluten-free grain and tends to be easier to digest than wheat. This recipe is also much simpler to make than standard yeast-based bread recipes as it simply needs stirring and baking – no kneading or proving required. The roasted peppers and pine nuts provide a delicious Mediterranean flavour, but could easily be substituted by sun-blush tomatoes and walnuts or even pumpkin or sunflower seeds.

SERVES 12 (freezes well)

150g (5oz) fine cornmeal/polenta

150g (5oz) cashew nuts, ground in a food processor (or use an extra 150g/5^1/2oz cornmeal if avoiding nuts)

1 tsp sea salt

3 tsp baking powder

225ml (7^1/2fl oz) semi-skimmed milk (or oat or rice milk)

3 medium free-range or organic eggs

5 tbsp mild olive oil

150g (5oz) roasted peppers in oil, drained and finely chopped

2 heaped tbsp pine nuts

1 Preheat the oven to 200°C/400°F/gas mark 6. Line a baking tray (around 20 x 30cm/8 x 12in) with baking paper. (If you prefer a thicker cornbread, use a 20 x 20cm/8 x 8in tray.)

2 Place the cornmeal, ground cashews and salt in a mixing bowl and sieve the baking powder on top. Stir to mix thoroughly.

3 Stir the milk, eggs and oil together in a bowl or jug and pour into the dry ingredients. Add the peppers and stir to form a loose dough.

4 Pour the dough in to the prepared baking tray, scatter the pine nuts evenly over the top and bake for 25 minutes until golden on top and firm to the touch. Cool on a wire rack then cut into squares and store in an airtight container.

Cook's notes Allergy suitability: gluten/wheat/yeast/dairy free (if using non-dairy milk) • Vegetarian • Can be made in advance • Suitable for freezing

Sweet Potato Mash

Sweet potatoes get their beautiful orange colour from their beta-carotene content. Beta-carotene is converted into vitamin A, which is necessary for healthy skin and immunity as well as being of great importance for a healthy pregnancy (albeit not above a certain level). If you are planning pregnancy or are already pregnant, eating lots of beta-carotene-rich orange and yellow coloured fruits and vegetables helps your body safely maintain adequate vitamin A levels. You could also add a sliced carrot to the steamer and mash it with the potato. Sweet potato mash can be reheated for easy leftovers, or spread over cooked mince to make a very healthy and colourful shepherd's pie.

SERVES 4

4 medium–large sweet potatoes, peeled
A little sea salt
Freshly ground black pepper
Knob of butter or olive oil (optional)

1 Slice the sweet potatoes thinly and steam for around 12 minutes until soft.

2 Place in a pan and mash roughly then stir in the seasoning (and butter or oil if using, although sweet potatoes are naturally fairly creamy) to taste and warm through.

Cook's notes Allergy suitability: gluten/wheat/dairy/yeast free (if not adding butter) • Medium GL • Vegetarian • Can be made in advance

Braised Butternut Squash

Orange-fleshed vegetables like squashes are very high in the antioxidant vitamin beta-carotene, which the body then converts into vitamin A – a good, safe route to getting adequate vitamin A during pregnancy when there are toxicity issues with high levels from supplements and liver. This braised dish is wonderfully warming and is an ideal accompaniment to sausages. Vegetarians or vegans could combine it with quinoa for a complete, balanced meal.

SERVES 2

¹/₂ a medium butternut squash
1 tbsp coconut oil or mild olive oil
1 large red onion, finely chopped
¹/₂ tsp ground cinnamon
¹/₂ tsp ground ginger
¹/₂ tsp turmeric
500ml (17fl oz) vegetable stock
Freshly ground black pepper

1 Cut the squash into cubes (don't peel it, just scrape out the seeds). Heat the oil in a saucepan, add the onion and sweat for three to four minutes then add the squash and spices, stir and cook for another couple of minutes.

2 Pour in the stock, bring to the boil then cover and simmer for 30 minutes.

3 Uncover and simmer for a further 10 minutes or so to allow the squash to soften. Sprinkle with black pepper before serving.

Cook's notes Allergy suitability: gluten/wheat/dairy/yeast free (depending on the stock content) • Vegetarian • Can be made in advance • Suitable for freezing

Leeks in a Tahini White Sauce

This delicious, dairy-free sauce gets its rich, creamy flavour and texture from tahini – a paste of ground sesame seeds. It could not be simpler to make and is very good served with fish or chicken, or simply stir in a can of butterbeans to make a complete dish for vegetarians. Sesame seeds are a good source of calcium – a mineral which you will have higher requirements of during pregnancy.

SERVES 4

2 tsp coconut oil or mild olive oil

4 large leeks, rinsed and finely sliced

4 tbsp tahini

2 heaped tsp vegetable bouillon powder or similar

1 Heat the oil in a large saucepan and add the leeks. Sauté for a couple of minutes then cover and sweat for around five to 10 minutes until they soften.

2 Meanwhile, place the tahini, 125ml (4½fl oz) water and the bouillon powder in a small pan and stir together over a medium heat (don't worry if it curdles at this stage). Pour over the leeks and stir until it turns into a thick, creamy and smooth sauce.

3 Taste and check the seasoning – you can always add a little more bouillon powder or water – and stir to bring the sauce back to a thick, creamy consistency.

Cook's notes Allergy suitability: gluten/wheat/dairy free • Vegetarian

Quinoa with Roasted Vegetables

Although very similar in look and taste to couscous or bulghur wheat, quinoa is in fact the seed of a fruit from the Andes and is highly regarded for its excellent protein content. It also contains more calcium than milk, so try it where you might normally use couscous or bulghur wheat, to top up your levels of this pregnancy mineral. This recipe makes a very good accompaniment to the Tomato and Basil Chicken Patties on page 104. If you have any to hand, stick a sprig of rosemary in the roasting tin with the vegetables; it not only adds flavour but also has antibacterial and antioxidant properties.

SERVES 4

3 courgettes, cut into bite-size chunks

2 red onions, cut into wedges

3 red, yellow or orange peppers, cut into bite-size chunks

4 whole garlic cloves

2 tbsp mild olive oil

250g (9oz) quinoa

1 tsp sea salt

Good handful of fresh basil leaves, roughly torn or chopped

2 tbsp pine nuts (or pumpkin seeds)

100g (4oz) sun-blush tomatoes, finely chopped (optional)

2 tbsp extra virgin olive oil or oil from the sun-blush tomatoes (optional)

Freshly ground black pepper

Sprinkle of sea salt, to taste

1 Preheat the oven to 180°C/350°F/gas mark 4. Place the courgette, onion and pepper chunks and the garlic in a roasting tin. Drizzle with the oil, stir to coat evenly then place in the oven for around 45 minutes to an hour, taking the tray out and stirring halfway through to turn the vegetables.

2 Cook the quinoa with the salt according to the pack instructions (as a rule of thumb, cover with just over two parts water to one part quinoa, cover and simmer for around 10 minutes then leave to sit, covered, for a further five minutes to let the grains soak up all the water and fluff up). Reserve, covered, to keep warm.

3 When the vegetables are cooked (they should be soft when pierced), fold into the quinoa along with the basil, pine nuts, sun-blush tomatoes and oil if using, then season to taste.

Cook's notes Allergy suitability: gluten/wheat/dairy/yeast free • Vegetarian • Can be made in advance

Griddled Peppers and Courgettes

This is the perfect summer accompaniment to the Lamb Burgers on page 114 or the Wild Rice Salad with Rosemary Roasted Vegetables on page 135. Slices of pepper and courgette are lightly seared on the griddle pan – quite delicious – and the quick cooking time means that more vitamins and antioxidants are preserved.

SERVES 4

2 red peppers
4 medium courgettes
4 tbsp mild olive oil
Fresh basil to serve

1 Slice the peppers lengthways into fairly thick strips. Top and tail the courgettes then finely slice lengthways. This is easier and neater when done using a mandolin on the thinnest setting rather than a knife, but either works.

2 Place the pepper and courgette strips in a large bowl and pour the oil over them.

3 Preheat a griddle pan until very hot and smoking and get a large plate ready for the cooked vegetables. Add the peppers to the griddle and cook for around 15 minutes, turning halfway, until they are soft. Set to one side while you griddle the courgettes.

4 Fill the pan surface with strips of courgette, taking care not to let them overlap. When the pan is full up it will be time to turn over the first strips then move on to the later ones. If you have cut the courgettes more thickly then they may need a little longer to sear on the pan but they simply need to sear and cook a little – it doesn't take long but you have to stay at the hob and work fairly quickly.

Cook's notes Allergy suitability: gluten/wheat/dairy/yeast free • Vegetarian • Can be made in advance

Roasted Celeriac

Celeriac is an often under-used vegetable. Although it can be mashed or roasted like potatoes, in fact it has a much lower starch content, giving it a low glycemic load. It makes a delicious accompaniment to the Sausage, Olive and Vegetable Bake on page 110.

SERVES 4

1 medium celeriac
2 tbsp mild olive oil
Good pinch of sea salt

1 Preheat the oven to 190°C/375°F/gas mark 5.

2 Peel the celeriac or cut off its outer skin then cube. Place it in a roasting tin, drizzle with the oil and sprinkle the salt over the top. Shake and stir to coat evenly.

3 Roast for about an hour until soft and golden. Stir occasionally to turn and allow it to colour fairly evenly.

Cook's notes Allergy suitability: gluten/wheat/dairy/yeast free • Vegetarian

Coleslaw

This crunchy, refreshing coleslaw is a mixture of nutrient-packed vegetables, from beta-carotene-rich carrots to sulphur-containing red onion and cruciferous cabbage. Mixing mayonnaise with live yoghurt helps to keep the fat content low.

SERVES 4–6 (keeps in the fridge for a couple of days).

275g (10oz) white cabbage
1 apple, cored but unpeeled
1 small red onion
2 large carrots (topped, tailed and peeled if not organic)
2 tbsp live natural yoghurt
1–2 tbsp mayonnaise

1 Finely grate the cabbage, apple, onion and carrots in a food processor (or use a manual grater if necessary).

2 Tip into a large bowl and stir in the yoghurt and mayonnaise until evenly coated. Taste and add a little more mayonnaise if preferred, but I think using more yoghurt to mayo gives the mixture a pleasingly tart flavour.

Cook's notes Allergy suitability: gluten/wheat/yeast free • Vegetarian • Can be made in advance

Red Onion, Tomato, Avocado and Basil Salad

Colour is a great indicator of a plant's phyto-nutrient content: in general, the brighter the colour, the higher the level, so it makes sense to choose red onions over white, as in this salad. Raw red onions are also sweeter than white ones. This dish not only looks good, it is also carefully balanced; the fat content of the avocado actually helps your body to absorb the carotenoid antioxidants from the tomatoes.

SERVES 4

3 large ripe, vine tomatoes
1 small red onion
2 ripe avocados
Good squeeze of lemon juice
Freshly ground black pepper
A little sea salt (optional)
Handful of fresh basil leaves, roughly torn

1 Cut the tomatoes into very fine slices and arrange on a plate or platter.

2 Slice the onion very finely (a mandolin makes this very quick and easy to do) and scatter over the tomatoes. De-stone the avocados and slice the flesh lengthways then scoop out of the shell and lay the slices on top.

3 Sprinkle with lemon juice, black pepper, a little salt and the torn basil.

Cook's notes Allergy suitability: gluten/wheat/dairy/yeast free • Vegetarian • Can be made in advance (but add the basil just before serving)

Teatime Treats

If, like many women, you struggle to control a sweet tooth, you can relax and enjoy the following recipes as a teatime treat or snack. These treats are packed with whole foods, from wholemeal flour and ancient grains like spelt, to nuts and seeds and fresh and dried fruit, plus spices that provide nutritional benefits as well as flavour. They're a far cry from refined, sugary cakes and biscuits, and contribute valuable fibre, vitamins, minerals and antioxidants to your diet, as well as appealing to your taste buds.

You will notice that I often use sugar alternatives such as xylitol and agave syrup as well as fresh and dried fruit to sweeten the recipes. These are intended to limit the disruption to blood sugar balance that comes from standard sweeteners like sugar and golden syrup. This makes them less fattening and less likely to disturb energy and concentration levels. In fact you would need to eat nine spoonfuls of xylitol for the same impact on blood sugar levels as just one spoonful of sugar! This does not give you a completely free rein to gorge on sweet things, however, as although preferable to standard sweeteners, they will do nothing to discourage a sweet tooth and excessive amounts of xylitol, for example, can upset bowels. They are used in the same quantity as standard sugar or syrup

and I have also given sugar or syrup options in brackets in case you prefer to use them, or if you cannot get hold of xylitol (see Resources, page 187 for more information).

Some of these recipes are flagged as being medium GL and a couple are high GL. This is due to the level of dried fruit used which, although extremely nutritious (being stuffed with fibre, vitamins, minerals and antioxidants), is nonetheless a concentrated source of fruit sugars and so will raise blood sugar levels. This is not a problem when enjoyed occasionally. Nonetheless they should be consumed in moderation only, particularly if you are trying to lose weight and balance blood sugar prior to conceiving.

Banana Flapjack Bites

These soft, chewy biscuits are naturally free from wheat, dairy, refined sugar and added fat.

MAKES 6 (ingredients can be doubled to make a bigger batch)

2 tbsp agave syrup (or honey or golden syrup)

2 tbsp tahini

100g (4oz) whole rolled oats

50g (2oz) ground almonds

1 ripe banana, mashed

1 Preheat the oven to 170°C/325°F/gas mark 3. Line a baking tray with baking paper.

2 Mix all of the ingredients together in a mixing bowl to form a sticky mixture.

3 Shape into six balls and place on the baking tray. Bake for around 25–30 minutes or until just turning golden on top. Leave to harden and cool on a wire rack.

Cook's notes Allergy suitability: wheat/dairy/yeast free • Vegetarian • Can be made in advance • Suitable for freezing

Applejack Slices

These soft, buttery slices of apple flapjack are rich in soluble fibre from both the oats and the apples, which helps digestion. They make a delicious teatime treat.

SERVES 8

2 unpeeled Bramley apples, coarsely grated

150g (5oz) slightly salted butter, softened, or coconut oil

4 tbsp agave syrup (or golden syrup)

200g (7oz) whole rolled oats

100g (4oz) ground almonds (for nut-free version omit and increase oats by 100g/4oz)

100g (4oz) xylitol (or soft brown sugar)

4 tsp mixed spice or cinnamon (optional)

1 Preheat the oven to 170°C/325°F /gas mark 3. Grease or line a 20cm/8in cake tin.

2 Gently stew the grated apple in a saucepan for a couple of minutes to soften. Add the butter, oil or margarine plus the syrup and melt together, taking care not to let the mixture boil. Stir in the oats, almonds and xylitol or sugar and spice and taste to check the flavour.

3 Spoon the mixture evenly into the cake tin, then bake for around 30 minutes or until just turning golden on top. Leave to harden and cool on a wire rack before slicing.

Cook's notes Allergy suitability: wheat/dairy free (if using oil) • Vegetarian • Can be made in advance • Suitable for freezing

Apricot and Ginger Flapjack Bites

Apricots are not only a good source of fibre, they are also rich in beta-carotene, a plant source of vitamin A, which safely tops up your levels of this essential baby-making nutrient. Choose unsulphured ones, which are not bright orange, to avoid potentially allergenic preservatives. The stem ginger provides sweetness and a warming flavour, plus ginger is known for its anti-nausea properties, so these bite-sized flapjacks would make an ideal treat for anyone suffering from morning sickness.

MAKES 10 (ingredients can be doubled to make a bigger batch)

50g (2oz) dried unsulphured apricots

75g (3oz) stem ginger in syrup, drained

75g (3oz) butter, coconut oil or non-dairy margarine

1 tbsp agave syrup (or golden syrup)

100g (4oz) whole rolled oats

50g (2oz) ground almonds

1 Preheat the oven to 170°C/325°F/gas mark 3. Line a baking tray with baking paper.

2 Very finely chop or blend the apricots and ginger together to make a mushy paste then place in a small saucepan with the butter, oil or margarine and syrup and gently melt, taking care not to let it boil.

3 Stir in the oats and almonds to coat evenly. Allow to cook slightly.

4 Shape the mixture into 10 walnut-sized balls and place on the baking tray. Bake for around 20 minutes or until just turning golden on top. Leave to harden and cool on a wire rack.

Cook's notes Allergy suitability: wheat/dairy free (if not using butter) • Vegetarian • Can be made in advance • Suitable for freezing

Chocolate Biscuit Cake

This rich and chewy fridge cake needs no cooking and, despite its rich, decadent taste, is much healthier than a standard chocolate biscuit cake. Instead of golden syrup, naturally low-GL agave syrup and tahini are used to bind the mixture together, and in place of digestive biscuits unsweetened oat cakes are used. The seeds also add protein and minerals. This cake is ideal for afternoon tea or as an after-supper treat with a cup of mint tea. It keeps for ages and can even be frozen – I like to eat it straight from the freezer, like a chocolate ice cream bar!

SERVES 10

200g (7oz) good-quality dark chocolate (around 70 per cent cocoa solids)

50g (2oz) tahini

1 tbsp agave syrup (or honey or golden syrup)

150g (5oz) plain coarse-milled oat cakes, broken into pieces

100g (4oz) goji berries, mixed dried fruit or sultanas

50g (2oz) pumpkin seeds

50g (2oz) sunflower seeds

2 tsp ground mixed spice

1 tsp ground cinnamon

1 Grease or line a 20cm (8in) cake tin.

2 Break the chocolate into pieces and melt over a bain marie. (Half fill a saucepan with water and let simmer. Place the chocolate in a bowl over the saucepan, making sure the base of the bowl does not touch the water, and let the chocolate gently melt over the heat, stirring occasionally).

3 When the chocolate is melted, turn off the heat but keep the chocolate in the bain marie so that the residual heat keeps it runny. Stir in the tahini and syrup until smooth then mix in the remaining ingredients until evenly coated.

4 Immediately spread the mixture evenly over the cake tin then pop in the fridge to chill and set for at least an hour, preferably two – or pop in the freezer for half an hour. Break into large chunks or cut into squares and store in a cake tin or freeze.

Cook's notes Allergy suitability: gluten/wheat/dairy free • Medium GL • Vegetarian • Can be made in advance • Suitable for freezing

Apple and Cinnamon Muffins

These soft, squidgy muffins are quite delicious and are bursting with flavour and natural sweetness from the apples and dried fruit. The wholemeal flour adds texture plus considerably more B vitamins and essential minerals than refined flour. You could also serve these muffins warm as a pudding, with custard or a little vanilla ice cream.

MAKES 8

2 medium Bramley apples

75g (3oz) butter, softened, or coconut oil or non-dairy margarine

100g (4oz) xylitol (or soft brown sugar)

120ml (4fl oz) semi-skimmed milk (or oat or almond milk)

2 medium organic or free-range eggs

1 tsp vanilla extract

4 tsp ground cinnamon

150g (5oz) plain wholemeal flour

1 tsp baking powder

1 tsp bicarbonate of soda

75g (3oz) dried mixed fruit

25g (1oz) pumpkin seeds

1 Preheat the oven to 180°C/350°F/gas mark 4. Line a muffin tray with eight muffin cases or place the cases on a baking sheet.

2 Core and dice the apples (but leave unpeeled for added fibre). Stew the diced apple with a splash of water in a covered pan for around five minutes, so that it just starts to soften.

3 Cream the butter, oil or margarine with the xylitol or sugar until soft and creamy.

4 Blend or mix in the milk, eggs, vanilla extract, cinnamon, flour, baking powder and bicarbonate of soda until smooth, then stir in the dried mixed fruit at the end. Spoon the mixture evenly into the eight muffin moulds. Sprinkle the tops with seeds.

5 Bake for around 30 minutes or until the muffins have risen and the tops are golden and relatively firm to the touch. Remove from the oven and leave to cool in the moulds to help them hold their shape.

Cook's notes Allergy suitablility: dairy free (if using coconut oil or non-dairy margarine) • Vegetarian • Medium GL • Can be made in advance • Suitable for freezing

Fruit Cake

This absolutely delicious cake gets its natural sweetness from the fruit, with no added sugar. The high level of fruit sugars raises the cake's glycemic load but fruit is at least an unrefined sweetener and is also a very rich source of fibre, vitamins and minerals. It is wonderful served warm as pudding with custard or cold at teatime. If your health food shop doesn't stock Rooibos Chai (a caffeine-free tea with a blend of cinnamon, ginger, cardamom, chicory, cloves, black pepper and citrus peel), plain Rooibos (also known as Redbush) tea will also work.

SERVES 10

575g (1lb 5oz) mixed dried fruit

1 small apple, unpeeled, grated

275ml (9fl oz) hot Rooibos Chai tea

150g (5oz) slightly salted butter, coconut oil or dairy-free margarine suitable for baking

100g (4oz) ground almonds

200g (7oz) wholemeal self-raising flour

1 tsp baking powder

3 tsp mixed spice

3 large free-range or organic eggs, beaten

100g (4oz) flaked almonds, finely chopped

4 drops almond extract (not artificial almond essence), or to taste

1 Put the dried fruit and apple into a bowl, cover with the hot tea (leave the bag in) and allow to the fruit to infuse and plump up for a couple of hours (or an hour at least). Take the butter or margarine out of the fridge to soften to room temperature.

2 Preheat the oven to 170°C/325°F/gas mark 3. Grease and line a 20cm(8in) cake tin.

3 Cream the butter, oil or margarine with the ground almonds until smooth.

4 Sieve the flour, baking powder and mixed spice into a separate bowl. Next, gradually add half of the flour mixture and all of the eggs to the creamed butter mixture.

5 Fold the chopped almonds, almond extract and fruit (removing the tea bag) into the mixture then finally fold in the remaining flour to give a soft dropping consistency.

6 Pour the mixture into the cake tin then bake for around an hour or until a skewer comes out clean and the top is golden and firm to the touch. Allow to cool in the tin then store in an airtight container or freeze.

Cook's notes Allergy suitability: dairy free (if using coconut oil or a dairy-free margarine) • Vegetarian • High GL • Can be made in advance • Suitable for freezing

Blueberry Tea Bread

There is no added sugar in this loaf, which gets its flavour from the naturally sweet bananas and blueberries. If you want to make it sweeter add a large handful of dried fruit such as dried mixed peel or serve it with some pure fruit jam or compote (one with no added sugar) – blueberry compote is absolutely delicious on this. This tea bread is ideal for an afternoon snack that won't send your blood sugar rocketing. It is best made the day before eating to let the flavours develop.

MAKES 1 LOAF (around 10 thick slices)

225g (8oz) plain wholemeal flour

¾ tsp bicarbonate of soda

4 ripe, medium-sized bananas, mashed

150g (5oz) blueberries

2 medium free-range or organic eggs, lightly beaten

100ml (3fl oz) mild olive oil

1 tsp vanilla extract

75g (3oz) chopped walnuts

3 tsp ground cinnamon

1 Line a 900g (2lb) loaf tin with baking paper. Preheat the oven to 150°C/300°F/gas mark 2.

2 Sift the flour and bicarbonate of soda together (tip in any leftover bran from the flour) into a mixing bowl. Add the remaining ingredients and stir together to form a thick batter.

3 Pour into the lined loaf tin and bake for around an hour and 15 minutes, or until the top feels fairly hard and the mixture doesn't wobble when the tin is shaken. Leave to cool on a wire rack before storing in an airtight container.

Cook's notes Allergy suitability: dairy/yeast free • Vegetarian • Can be made in advance • Suitable for freezing

Spiced Walnut, Fruit and Spelt Bread

Spelt is an ancient cousin of wheat but it is far easier to digest and less likely to inflame irritable bowel symptoms or similar digestion problems. You can buy it from health food shops and good supermarkets. This teatime recipe is very simple to make as it does not require kneading or proving. It combines naturally sweet dried fruit with warming spices plus walnuts to provide a little added protein and crunch. Again the dried fruit makes this relatively high GL, but this dish is packed with nutrients and a much healthier choice than a shop-bought cake or tea bread.

SERVES 8–12

200g (7oz) spelt flour

100g (4oz) roughly chopped walnuts

4 tsp ground cinnamon

50g (2oz) xylitol (or brown sugar)

4 tsp baking powder

225ml (7¹/₂fl oz) semi-skimmed milk (or oat or rice milk)

3 medium free-range or organic eggs

5 tbsp mild olive oil

150g (5oz) mixed dried fruit

100g (4oz) walnuts to sprinkle on top

1 Preheat the oven to 200°C/400°F/gas mark 6. Line a 20 × 30cm (8 × 12in) baking tray with baking paper.

2 Place the spelt flour, chopped walnuts, cinnamon and xylitol or sugar in a mixing bowl and scatter the baking powder on top. Stir to mix thoroughly.

3 Stir the milk, eggs and oil together in a bowl or jug and pour into the dry ingredients along with the dried fruit, stirring to form a loose dough.

4 Pour into the prepared baking tray, sprinkle with the walnuts and bake for 25 minutes until golden on top and firm to the touch. Cool on a wire rack then cut into squares and store in an airtight container.

Cook's notes Allergy suitability: yeast/dairy free (if using non-dairy milk) • Medium GL • Vegetarian • Can be made in advance • Suitable for freezing

Carrot, Orange and Poppy Seed Loaf

This soft, squidgy tea bread is full to the brim with the flavours of citrus, sweet carrot and warming ginger. Enjoy a slice for afternoon tea and feel smug in the knowledge that you are topping up your fibre levels plus providing vitamins and minerals from the wholefood ingredients. Choose organic or unwaxed oranges to avoid pesticides and wax, and really scrape out the shells with a spoon to get all the juice.

MAKES 1 LOAF (around 10 thick slices)

225g (8oz) plain wholemeal flour

1 tsp bicarbonate of soda

2 tsp ground ginger

3 tsp cinnamon

2 large carrots, peeled (if non-organic) and grated

100g (4oz) sultanas

Zest and juice of 2 large organic or unwaxed oranges

90ml (3fl oz) mild olive oil

50g (2oz) xylitol (or soft brown sugar)

2 large free-range or organic eggs, lightly beaten

50g (2oz) poppy seeds

1 Line a loaf tin (around 22 × 12 × 6.5cm/8½ × 4½ × 2½in) with baking paper. Preheat the oven to 150°C/300°F/gas mark 2.

2 Sift the flour, bicarbonate of soda, ginger and cinnamon into a mixing bowl (tip any leftover grains from the flour back into the mixture). Add the remaining ingredients and stir well until it is all mixed together then scrape into the prepared tin.

3 Bake in the centre of the oven for around an hour and 15 minutes, or until the top feels fairly hard and the mixture doesn't wobble when the tin is shaken. Leave to cool on a wire rack before storing in an airtight container.

Cook's notes Allergy suitability: dairy/yeast free • Vegetarian • Medium GL • Can be made in advance • Suitable for freezing

Puddings

These puddings are unashamedly bursting with nutritious ingredients, such as wholemeal flour, fruit, nuts, live yoghurt and spices, and give the option to use dairy-free ingredients like olive and coconut oil where possible to make them suitable for people avoiding dairy products. They, nonetheless, remain absolutely scrumptious and have been enjoyed by countless friends and family, standing up to scrutiny from anyone suspicious of anything 'too healthy'. They can all be enjoyed as a teatime treat as well as being served as a pudding. Some of the recipes, like Banana Split with Chocolate Hazelnut Sauce on page 170 or the Frozen Fruit Smoothie on page 174, can be thrown together in minutes – for when you have a sudden urge for a pudding or are short on time or energy.

Like the Teatime Treats recipes, I often use sugar alternatives such as xylitol and agave syrup as well as fruit as sweeteners, and you'll notice that a couple of these recipes are flagged as being Medium GL. This is not a problem when enjoyed occasionally and will help to fill you up if you are pregnant and feeling ravenous due to your increased calorie requirements, but they nonetheless should be consumed in moderation, particularly if you are trying to lose weight and balance blood sugar prior to conceiving.

Chocolate Carrot Cake

A sticky, squidgy cake that is bound to be a hit whether served for afternoon tea or as a rich pudding with live natural yoghurt or vanilla ice cream. I have replaced refined white flour and sugar with fibre-rich wholemeal flour, while the walnuts add protein and valuable minerals like zinc and magnesium.

SERVES 10

170g (6oz) good-quality dark chocolate

200g (7oz) self-raising wholemeal flour

2 tsp ground mixed spice

100g (4oz) xylitol (or soft brown sugar)

225g (8oz) carrots, grated

Finely grated zest of 2 large organic or unwaxed oranges

55g (2oz) walnuts or hazelnuts, finely chopped (or omit for a nut-free version)

180ml (6fl oz) mild olive oil or extra virgin rapeseed oil

2 medium free-range or organic eggs

Icing

2 tbsp cocoa powder or cacao

2 tbsp mild olive oil or extra virgin rapeseed oil

2 tbsp agave syrup (or golden syrup)

1 Preheat the oven to 180°C/350°F/gas mark 4. Line a 20cm/8in loose-bottomed cake tin with baking paper and grease the sides.

2 Melt the chocolate in a bain marie. (Half fill a saucepan with water and let simmer. Place the chocolate in a heat-proof bowl on the saucepan, making sure the base of the bowl does not touch the water, and let the chocolate gently melt over the heat). Alternatively, melt it in a microwave.

3 Sift the flour and mixed spice into a bowl. Stir in the xylitol or sugar, grated carrots, orange zest and nuts. Make a well in the centre, pour in the oil and add the eggs. Beat the eggs into the oil then fold into the rest of the mixture in the bowl.

4 Stir in the melted chocolate and pour the mixture into the prepared cake tin. Bake for around 25–30 minutes, or until the cake is just firm to the touch and a skewer inserted comes out clean – it is such a squidgy, moist cake that it will still appear very soft and gooey when cooked. Allow to cool on a wire rack before icing.

5 Place the cocoa, oil and syrup in a small pan and heat gently for 30–60 seconds or so as you stir them together until combined. Spread on the cake and allow to cool and set before storing in an airtight container.

Cook's notes Allergy suitablility: dairy free (check that the dark chocolate is dairy free) • Vegetarian • Medium GL • Suitable for freezing (ice after defrosting) • Can be made in advance

Chocolate Chestnut Torte

This flourless cake is gluten and dairy free and has no added fat or sugar aside from that in the chocolate (use a good-quality 70 per cent cocoa solids chocolate). It still manages to remain rich and moist, however, and would make an excellent dinner party pudding. Chestnuts supply slow-releasing carbohydrate along with trace minerals and very little fat. You could also use unsweetened chestnut purée. Serve this torte warm or at room temperature, with strawberries or raspberries and a dollop of live natural yoghurt, which works better than ice cream as its tart acidity balances the rich chocolate.

SERVES 8

100g (4oz) dark chocolate (70% cocoa solids)

100g (4oz) roasted, ready-to-use chestnuts

3 medium free-range or organic eggs, separated

Zest and juice of 1 large organic or unwaxed orange

1/2 tsp baking powder

Live natural yoghurt, to serve (optional)

1 Preheat the oven to 180°C/350°F/gas mark 4. Line a round, loose-bottomed cake tin (around 20cm/8in in diameter) with baking paper and grease the sides.

2 Melt the chocolate in a bain marie. (Half fill a saucepan with water and let simmer. Place the chocolate in a heat-proof bowl on the saucepan, making sure the base of the bowl does not touch the water, and let the chocolate gently melt over the heat). Alternatively, melt it in a microwave.

3 Finely grind the chestnuts in a food processor and add the rest of the ingredients, apart from the egg whites. Blend ingredients together until smooth and well combined.

4 Beat the egg whites until just stiff and gently fold into the chocolate mixture using a large metal spoon. Pour into the prepared tin, place on a baking sheet, smooth out the top and bake for around 30 minutes or until the top is cracked and hard to the touch and a skewer comes out clean. Remove from the oven and cool in the tin. Serve warm or at room temperature.

Cook's notes Allergy suitability: gluten/wheat/yeast free/dairy (check that the dark chocolate is dairy free if necessary) • Vegetarian • Can be made in advance • Suitable for freezing

Banana Split with Chocolate Hazelnut Sauce

This deliciously satisfying pudding can be thrown together in minutes. It will hit the spot if you are craving chocolate while also topping up your intake of fibre, for digestion, and protein to help your baby's growth. Cacao – raw, unprocessed chocolate powder – is available from good health food shops, along with hazelnut butter. Cacao is incredibly rich in beneficial minerals, while the agave syrup has a very low glycemic load so it won't upset your blood sugar levels. You could serve with ice cream instead of yoghurt if wished.

SERVES 2

Sauce
3 tbsp unsalted hazelnut butter

3 tbsp raw cacao powder (or ordinary cocoa powder)

2 tbsp agave syrup (or golden syrup or honey)

3 tbsp water

2 bananas

4 heaped tbsp live natural yoghurt

1 heaped tbsp unblanched hazelnuts

1 Mix the sauce ingredients together with a fork, and add enough water to make a smooth, fairly thick sauce – about three tablespoons. Taste to check the sweetness and adjust if necessary. You can also add more water to make it thinner if wished.

2 Peel the bananas, split each one in half lengthways and place in two bowls. Spoon the yoghurt on top of each banana then add the chocolate hazelnut sauce.

3 Finish with a sprinkle of roughly chopped hazelnuts and serve immediately.

Cook's notes Allergy suitability: gluten/wheat free • Vegetarian • Medium GL

Plum and Ginger Fool

This thick, creamy fool is delicious. Use a reduced-fat Greek yoghurt if you wish to make this lower in saturated fat. The ginger adds a warming flavour as well as anti-nausea, antioxidant and antibacterial properties.

SERVES 2

500g (1lb 2oz) plums
1/2 tsp ground ginger, or to taste
75–100g (3–4oz) xylitol (or caster sugar)
275g (10oz) Greek yoghurt

1 Stone and roughly chop the plums and place them in a saucepan with a splash of water, the ginger and xylitol or sugar (adjust the quantity according to the sweetness of the plums and your taste buds). Cover and simmer gently for around 15 minutes so that the fruit softens. Set aside to cool.

2 When it is cold, drain the fruit and reserve the syrup. Blend the plums until smooth in a food processor or with a hand-held blender.

3 Return the reserved syrup to the pan and heat to reduce it by half. Stir it into the plum purée and again allow to cool.

4 Next fold the plum mixture into the yoghurt to form a smooth, thick fool.

5 Spoon into individual glasses or a large serving dish and refrigerate until ready to serve.

Cook's notes Allergy suitability: gluten/wheat free • Can be made in advance

Plum Crumble with Cinnamon and Oats

A sticky, sweet, proper pud that is lighter on the digestive system and less fattening than traditional versions thanks to the use of oats and almonds for the crumble topping rather than refined flour. To make this nut free, simply replace the almonds with another 100g/4oz of oats. You can also make this dairy and sugar free by using coconut oil or a dairy-free margarine (choose one that is free from hydrogenated fats) instead of butter and xylitol in place of sugar. Cinnamon adds a delicious warming flavour that complements the plums perfectly, as well as helping your body to keep blood sugar levels in check.

SERVES 6

Crumble
200g (7oz) whole rolled oats
100g (4oz) ground almonds
75g (3oz) xylitol (or soft brown sugar)
100g (4oz) softened butter, coconut oil or
 dairy-free margarine

Filling
1kg (2.2lb) plums, halved and stoned
3 tsp ground cinnamon
100g (4oz) xylitol (or soft brown sugar)

1 Preheat the oven to 180°C/350°F/gas mark 4.

2 Whiz half the oats in a food processor to grind into flour. Add the ground almonds, xylitol or sugar and butter, coconut oil or margarine and blitz again to form crumbs. Stir in the remaining oats.

3 Place the plums in the base of a medium to large baking dish. Scatter with the cinnamon and xylitol or sugar, top with the crumble mixture and even out the surface. Bake for 40–60 minutes or until the top starts to turn golden brown and the fruit is soft.

Cook's notes Allergy suitability: wheat/yeast/dairy free (if not using butter) • Vegetarian • Suitable for freezing • Can be made in advance (chill until ready to cook)

Stewed Apple with Lemon

This recipe is very quick and easy to fling together and keeps well in the fridge or freezer, making it ideal for batch-cooking. The lemon zest lifts the simple stewed fruit to something much tastier. It also contributes the antioxidant limonene to protect cells from damage. Leaving the peel on the apples boosts the fibre content to help your digestion, while using xylitol keeps this pudding sugar free.

SERVES 4

675g (1½lb) Bramley apples
160g (5½oz) xylitol (or soft brown sugar)
Finely chopped zest of ½ an organic or
  unwaxed lemon

1 Core and slice the apples and put them in a saucepan with a good splash of water, cover and bring to the boil then add the xylitol or sugar and lemon zest.

2 Simmer uncovered, over a low heat, for around 10 minutes or until the apple slices are soft and disintegrating. Stir from time to time and add a splash more water if they start to stick and burn.

3 Served warm or cold, on its own or with custard, ice cream or live natural yoghurt.

Cook's notes Allergy suitability: gluten/wheat/dairy/yeast free • Vegetarian • Can be made in advance • Suitable for freezing

Frozen-fruit Smoothie

If you are craving ice cream or sorbet (off limits during pregnancy due to the raw egg whites) this honestly tastes just as good but is amazingly healthy, being free from added sugar and bursting with vitamin C and flavonoids from the berries. It takes just one minute to make.

SERVES 1

100g (4oz) frozen mixed berries
60ml (2fl oz) semi-skimmed milk (or oat or
  rice milk)
1 small, fairly ripe banana

1 Blend all of the ingredients together until smooth and the consistency of sorbet or frozen yoghurt.

2 Add more milk or berries to adjust the thickness if wished, then serve immediately before it melts.

Cook's notes Allergy suitability: gluten/wheat/dairy free (if using a non-dairy milk) • Vegetarian

Drinks

Never before has what you drink become so important – or so contentious. You will of course be aware of the need to avoid or at the very least dramatically restrict your caffeine and alcohol intake during pregnancy, but it is also worthy of consideration before you even conceive. Both alcohol and caffeine can deplete B vitamins, which are vital for hormone balance, not to mention energy production and coping with stress. If you regularly consume caffeine or alcohol, cutting down consumption before you conceive will also make it far easier to abstain during pregnancy, when the implications become far more serious. A high intake of caffeine has been linked to low birth weight and even miscarriage (see Chapter 4, page 36 for more information). Alcohol during pregnancy can cause Foetal Alcohol Syndrome – the biggest cause of non-genetic mental handicap in the Western world. For this reason, the standard advice during pregnancy is to abstain from alcohol completely (see page 23).

To make it easier to abstain from caffeine and alcohol, this section includes some tempting drinks that are not only safe during pregnancy but in many instances will also help to nourish your body. It covers everything from non-alcoholic cocktails, soft drinks and caffeine-free hot drinks, to juices and smoothies.

Time for Tea

Here are some caffeine-free (or, in the case of the green and white teas, very low caffeine) hot drinks to try. You can find many herbal teas in supermarkets nowadays, but if you are not having much luck try a health food shop.

- Peppermint – to ease digestion.

- Chamomile – to help relaxation and sleep.

- Redbush (also known as rooibos) – a South African leaf tea that is naturally caffeine free and particularly rich in antioxidants. It makes a good alternative to black tea as it is full flavoured, has a similarly strong brick-red colour and can be drunk with milk.

- Green tea – the secret behind green tea's reputation as a miracle medicine is its polyphenols, which are powerful antioxidants. These are also thought to help avoid blood clots (an increased risk during pregnancy).

- White tea (made from immature tea leaves) – even richer in health-boosting antioxidants than green tea and lower in caffeine. Let the water come off the boil before pouring over the tea to avoid damaging the delicate flavour.

- Honey and lemon in hot water – a great natural remedy for a sore throat. Use freshly squeezed lemon juice for a pure shot of vitamin C and Manuka honey for its strongly antibacterial, medicinal properties.

- Ginger, lemon and green tea – ginger is a very effective antidote to morning sickness and this vitamin C- and antioxidant-rich brew will also help soothe a cold or sore throat. Add two thin slices of fresh ginger root (no need to peel) and the juice of quarter or half a lemon (to taste) to a cup of green tea and infuse for a few minutes.

- Hot apple and ginger juice – place a mugful of pure (unsweetened) apple juice in a pan with a couple of slices of fresh root ginger. Cover and simmer very gently for 10 minutes to let the ginger infuse then remove the ginger and pour the juice into a mug.

- Raspberry leaf tea – traditionally used to tone the uterus in preparation for labour. Although opinions vary on when to start taking it, advice tends to be at around 34 weeks. Use loose leaf tea rather than tea bags (this is harder to find, although it can be bought from herbalists like Neals Yard or online) and brew a teaspoonful for around five minutes then discard before drinking. Postnatally, it is thought to help reduce bleeding, help the uterus return to its pre-pregnancy size and encourage milk production.

Juices and Smoothies

Freshly made fruit and vegetable juices are, of course, incredibly good sources of vitamins, minerals, antioxidants, enzymes, fibre and other plant nutrients. They are also very easy to digest and absorb. Don't go too mad on fruit juices, however; the juicing process extracts the fruit sugars and discards the fibre, so the sugar is absorbed far more quickly than if you were to eat the whole fruit. Smoothies are generally more filling as they blend the whole fruit, including the fibre, which helps to slow the sugar release and fill you up for longer, as well as helping digestion.

If you make juices regularly it is worth investing in a decent juicing machine as they have stronger motors to withstand regular, heavy use, and extract more juice and therefore more nutrients. Smoothies can simply be made with a cheap hand-held blender.

Choose organic or unsprayed fruit and vegetables in order to limit your exposure to potentially toxic pesticides and waxes. Such produce is also likely to be richer in vitamins and minerals than intensively produced fruits and vegetables. You should also thoroughly wash all ingredients that do not need peeling. If you are not using organic produce, you can spray and rinse fruit and vegetables with a 'veggie wash' (available from health food shops) to remove some of the pesticide residue.

You can blend banana or live natural yoghurt to thicken drinks. Other ways to add a creamy consistency include coconut milk or non-dairy milks such as unsweetened rice, soya, almond and oat milks. On page 179 you'll find a couple of ideas to get you started and to inspire you to create your own favourites.

Hot Chocolate

Sometimes there is nothing more relaxing than a cup of hot chocolate or cocoa. Swap refined drinking chocolate or cocoa powder for unprocessed, raw cacao powder. This avoids the added sugar and you will benefit from the many nutrients in the cocoa bean, such as magnesium and tryptophan (an amino acid that is converted into serotonin to give you the feel good factor). For anyone avoiding dairy products, this recipe is actually very good with oat or almond milk.

SERVES 1

250ml (8fl oz) semi-skimmed milk (or oat or almond milk)

2 heaped tsp cacao powder (or ordinary cocoa powder)

3 tsp xylitol (or sugar), to taste

Sprinkle of ground mixed spice or cinnamon (optional)

1 Gently heat all the milk, cacao and xylitol in a small saucepan for around five minutes until a pleasant drinking temperature but not too hot, whisking to combine.

2 Taste and adjust the sweetness if necessary. Serve sprinkled with the mixed spice or cinnamon if using.

Cook's notes Allergy suitability: gluten/wheat/yeast/dairy free (if using a non-dairy milk) • Vegetarian

Gingerade

Ginger is a brilliant remedy for morning sickness during pregnancy, but has other health benefits as well, including having antibacterial, antiviral and anti-inflammatory properties.

SERVES 2 (tall glasses)

50g (2oz) chunk of fresh root ginger

1 heaped tbsp xylitol (or sugar)

300ml (1/2 pt) still water

300ml (1/2 pt) naturally sparking mineral water (not carbonated)

1 Cut the ginger into large chunks (no need to peel), then place it with the xylitol and still water in a pan and bring to the boil.

2 Cover and simmer for around 10 minutes, then remove from the heat and leave to cool before removing the ginger pieces.

3 Stir the infused liquid into the sparkling mineral water. Serve chilled with ice and a slice of lemon.

Cook's notes Allergy suitability: gluten/wheat/dairy/yeast free • Vegetarian • Can be made in advance (keep chilled)

Cooling Coconut Smoothie

This tropical tasting drink is very refreshing and filling. Bananas are a good source of the blood-pressure-lowering mineral potassium, plus fibre to aid digestion. Many people steer clear of coconut milk because of its high fat content, but in fact it is rich in a special kind of plant-based saturated fat which appears to be readily used as energy rather than being stored as fat.

SERVES 1

1 banana
Large handful of strawberries
150ml (5fl oz) coconut milk
3 ice cubes

1 Peel the banana and hull the strawberries. Shake the coconut milk can before opening, as it tends to separate.

2 Blend all the ingredients together and drink immediately.

Cook's notes Allergy suitability: gluten/wheat/dairy/yeast free • Vegetarian • Can be made in advance (keep chilled)

Watermelon Whizz

Watermelon, as the name suggests, is a great way to top up your fluid levels – particularly if you are not a fan of drinking plain water. As well as being an excellent source of vitamin C, the bright red flesh is also rich in beta-carotene to help you maintain vitamin A levels, and the seeds contain vitamin E, which will help you avoid stretch marks. This is absolutely delicious and incredibly refreshing. It also provides some nourishment if you are feeling very sick and cannot face food. In fact my sister practically lived off this when she was pregnant one summer and had terrible morning sickness.

SERVES 1 (short glass)

200g (7oz) rindless watermelon

1 Blend the watermelon flesh, seeds and all, until smooth.

2 Serve on its own or with ice or blend some ice with the watermelon for an instant chilled juice.

Cook's notes Allergy suitability: gluten/wheat/dairy/yeast free • Vegetarian • Can be made in advance (keep chilled)

Banana and Chocolate Milkshake

This is a milkshake with a difference. The addition of a protein powder like whey protein makes this far more filling and nutritious than an ordinary milkshake, to nourish your body. My husband Nick used to make me protein shakes during the first few weeks after I gave birth to Oliver and they seemed to help my milk supply noticeably, giving me a much-needed quick energy fix. Check that the packaging does not advise against use during pregnancy – some contain high doses of nutrients which may be contraindicated. And watch out for artificial additives and harmful sweeteners.

SERVES 1

1 large banana

1 scoop (30g) of chocolate-flavoured protein powder (see introduction)

Milk (or oat or rice milk)

1 tbsp cashew nuts or sunflower or pumpkin seeds

Blend all the ingredients together until smooth.

Cook's notes Allergy suitability: gluten/wheat/yeast/dairy free (if using non-dairy milk) • Vegetarian • Can be made in advance (keep chilled)

Sickness Settler

This strong-flavoured, refreshing drink is packed with vitamin C and is also designed to help soothe a troubled digestive tract. Ginger helps to assuage nausea, while pineapple contains the digestive enzyme bromelain, which helps you break down your food and also has strong anti-inflammatory properties. The lemon and ginger add a refreshingly zingy flavour.

SERVES 1

1 carrot

1 pear

2 thick slices of fresh pineapple

1/2 a lemon

1/4 tsp fresh root ginger

Push each ingredient through the juicer according to the manufacturer's instructions.

Cook's notes Allergy suitability: gluten/wheat/dairy/yeast free • Vegetarian • Can be made in advance (keep chilled).

Resources

Consultants, Services and Organisations

BABY AND CHILD FIRST AID COURSE

Developed in conjunction with some of the world's leading first aid and paediatric specialists, First Aid for Kids is a complete first aid course presented on an interactive CD-ROM or, for Australia only, a 90 minute DVD. The course covers all aspects of basic first aid and allows you to review, refresh and learn at your own pace, with exercises to practise and test skills. For more information or to order visit www.firstaidforkids.com or call 020 7854 2861.

BIOCHEMICAL TESTING

A range of biochemical tests to screen for hormone imbalances, digestive disorders and toxicity, including hair mineral analysis, can be arranged via a Nutritional Therapist (see page 182).

A home homocysteine test can be ordered from YorkTest Laboratories, with full instructions provided to reduce levels if above optimal. At the time of going to press, the cost is £80. Visit www.yorktest.com or call freephone 0800 074 6185 for details. Also see www.thehfactor.com for information about other labs and supplements.

FORESIGHT

The preconceptual care charity has some useful information and provides access to a nationwide network of practitioners. For more information, visit www.foresight-preconception.org.uk

HYPNOBIRTHING

Highly recommended by Fiona! The Hypnobirthing Centre offers courses on the respected Mongan Method, teaching you and your birthing partner breathing and relaxation techniques to experience a more comfortable, calm and natural labour, and aims to reduce your need for medical intervention. Katherine Graves's holistic approach has made her courses very popular and she is highly regarded by London's top obstetricians. Courses are held across London plus several other locations. For more information visit www.thehypnobirthingcentre.co.uk or phone 0845 337 9149.

NATIONAL CHILDBIRTH TRUST (NCT)

The NCT is the UK's leading charity on pregnancy, birth and early parenthood. Every year the charity supports thousands of parents, offering information and support through a network of over 300 local branches, UK-wide helplines, antenatal and early days courses, breast-feeding counselling and peer support schemes. For more information visit www.nct.org.uk or phone the NCT Enquiries line on 0300 33 00 770.

NUTRITION CONSULTATIONS

For a personal referral by Patrick Holford to a nutritional therapist in your area, visit www.patrickholford.com and select 'consultations' for an immediate online referral. This service gives details of therapists in the UK and internationally. If there is no one available near by, you can always do an online assessment – see below.

NUTRITIONAL ASSESSMENT ONLINE

You can have your own personal health and nutrition assessment online. Visit www.patrickholford.com and look at the '100% Health Programme' section for details.

PRE-AND POST-NATAL THERAPIES

There are a number of complementary therapies that can be of huge benefit both before and after birth to aid the health and wellbeing of mother and baby. Reflexology and acupressure are particularly recommended in the late stages of pregnancy, to help the expectant mother to relax physically and mentally and encourage a natural delivery, while craniosacral therapy can be incredibly beneficial for newborns, particularly after a traumatic birth or for very fractious or distressed babies. Practitioner Ana Kolpy has great experience in all three disciplines and sees clients across London. She can be contacted via bodyworks@kolpy.f9.co.uk

PREGNANCY AND PAEDIATRIC CHIROPRACTIC

Pregnancy and paediatric chiropractic treatments help with back pain and other problems related to pregnancy as well as optimising the chances of a normal birth and helping with infant irritability, feeding or sleeping problems (often following a difficult birth). The McTimoney chiropractic method is incredibly gentle and safe, making it suitable during pregnancy. Registered McTimoney chiropractor Jane Cooke sees patients at her South and Central London clinics. Visit www.chiroclinic.info for more information.

SUSANNAH LAWSON DipION mBANT

Susannah is a nutritional therapist who has particular experience in preconceptual health and fertility for both men and women. As well as being the co-author of this book, she also wrote *Optimum Nutrition Before, During and After Pregnancy* with Patrick Holford (also published by Piatkus). She gives private consultations from her clinic in Hampshire. Contact her via www.susannah-lawson.co.uk

THE WOMEN'S NATURAL HEALTH PRACTICE

The Women's Natural Health Practice offers natural gynaecological, reproductive and obstetric health care for women. Diagnosis is based on both Western medicine and Chinese Medicine procedures while treatment is based on Traditional Chinese Medicine and naturopathic medicine only. Trevor Wing can be contacted on 0845 688 5270. Alternatively, email enquiries@naturalgynae.com or visit www.naturalgynae.com

Pregnancy and Baby Products

The following products are among Fiona's favourite items that she has come across during her research both for this book and for her own baby. They are all designed to help look after you and/or your baby's health or wellbeing.

BABY BATH

The special design of the original TummyTub® ensures babies relax in the familiar foetal position to make bath time enjoyable from birth. The design allows the baby to be immersed in the water up to shoulder level so that they feel warm, reassured and secure. The TummyTub helps babies settle and sleep, is especially recommended for premature babies and colicky babies and is widely used in hospitals. For more information or to order visit www.tummytub.co.uk

BABY CARRIERS

Babybjörn baby carriers have been designed in conjunction with paediatricians to ensure that they are comfortable for you and your baby, while also providing secure support for your child's spine and hips. The Babybjörn range also includes the Babysitter Balance, a rocker chair which helps the baby develop their motor skills and balance as well as soothing them. For more information or to order visit www.babybjorn.com

BABY HAMMOCKS

Hammock beds support an infant's early development, putting them in a womb-like, cradled position that aids sleep and soothes colic. They may also reduce the risk of 'flat head' syndrome. The Amby Nature's Nest is the only baby hammock to receive the JPMA and EC safety certification; visit www.amby.co.uk for more information or to order.

BABY SKIN CARE

Green Baby, winner of the Prima Baby and Pregnancy Awards 2009 for Best Children's Eco Range, produce organic, skin-friendly toiletries that are free from SLAs, SLSs, parabens and synthetic fragrances and preservatives, to protect your baby's sensitive skin. For more information or to order visit www.greenbaby.co.uk

BABY SLINGS

Sling carrying offers close contact for mother and baby to aid bonding and soothe babies, as well as allowing easy breast-feeding. The BabaSling is incredibly simple and comfortable to use in a number of different carrying positions. Its hammock style is perfectly shaped to support a newborn's developing spine and it can be adjusted easily to fit any adult. Visit www.thebabasling.co.uk. The Kari-Me has a unique harnessing system that allows parents to carry their babies safely and comfortably for long periods of time. It can be used in five different positions on babies from birth to up to 4 years old. Visit www.kari-me.com. Karma Baby pouch slings also enable you to carry your baby in comfort in several different positions and can be used from newborn until toddler. Visit www.mykarmababy.com. The ERGObaby carrier supports the baby's spine and promotes the healthiest position for a baby's hips whilst the ergonomic design supports the wearer's body. An insert for newborns makes this carrier suitable from birth onwards. Visit www.ergobabycarrier.com

BABY TOWELS

The Cuddledry is a unique apron-style towel for stress-free bath times, helping you to stay dry and lift your baby out of the bath easily. Made of organic unbleached cotton and natural bamboo fibre, the Cuddledry is soft, highly absorbent and fast drying, with naturally antibacterial properties. For more details or to order visit www.cuddledry.com

BIRTHING BALL

The Birth-ease birthing ball is ideal for use during pregnancy to relieve back pain and pregnancy discomfort, to help optimal foetal positioning for birth and for prenatal exercises to keep fit and build strength for labour, including for pelvic floor exercises. It is also invaluable during labour, when it can help you relax and cope with contractions, progress dilation and support active birth positions. For more information or to order visit www.birthease.co.uk

BISPHENOL-A (BPA) -FREE BREAST PUMPS AND BREAST-FEEDING ACCESSORIES

The number one choice of hospitals and mothers, the Medela range includes breast pumps, nursing pads and other breast-feeding accessories. All of its breast shields and collection containers/bottles have always been made of polypropylene, a durable BPA-free plastic. All existing research endorses the safety of polypropylene, whereas BPA is an industrial chemical that has been shown to be potentially harmful to human health. Order directly from Medela by telephoning 0870 950 5994 or visit www.medela.co.uk

BOLA PENDANTS

Mexican bolas are pendants for pregnant women that make soothing chimes as you walk or move to relax the baby. This easily recognisable sound will continue to soothe the baby after birth. Order online from www.BeanBabies.com

HEMP AND BAMBOO REUSABLE NAPPIES

MamaBless cloth nappies provide a good fit from birth to toddler and the adjustable fasteners make them just as quick to use as disposables. The eco-friendly fabric choices of hemp/organic cotton and cotton/bamboo are kinder on your baby's skin and have naturally antibacterial and antifungal properties to help prevent nappy rash. Uniquely, the MamaBless nappy can also be used as a trainer pant when your baby starts potty training. The MamaBless range also includes organic clothing and bedding. For more information or to order, visit www.mamabless.com

HOME BIRTH POOLS

Immersion in water is proven to make labour faster and easier, helping many women to cope better with pain and encouraging the hormones which are an integral part of a healthy birth. Birth Pool in a Box makes it possible for women to use water for their births at home, offering both Mini and Regular inflatable birth pools as well as kits to make set up and dismantling hassle free. Their new Eco pools are made from phthalate-free PVC, for a reduced impact on health and the environment. For more information or to order, visit www.birthpoolinabox.co.uk

LAMBSKIN BABY RUGS

Gabe and Grace supply high-quality Australian merino lambskins which are tanned especially for babies, without using harmful irritants such as chrome or formaldehyde. Lambskin helps to balance heat to keep babies cool in summer and snug in winter, and the specially cut length of the pile cushions and relieves pressure points, to comfort and soothe your child. The Gabe and Grace range includes pram liners, rugs, foot muffs and booties. Visit www.gabeandgrace.co.uk for more information or to order.

MATERNITY SUPPORT BELT

The patented Reenie maternity support belt by Emma Jane has been specifically designed to make pregnancy more comfortable by supporting your abdomen and relieving backache. The belt is unique in that it adjusts both at the back and front, to suit your changing shape. Recommended by hospitals and physiotherapists, and with nearly a quarter of a million sold worldwide each year, the Emma Jane support belt is the answer to backache during pregnancy – and after. Order online at www.emma-jane.com

NATURAL, SKIN-FRIENDLY MINERAL MAKE-UP

Known as The Skin Care Makeup, the Jane Iredale range of mineral make up is so safe and beneficial to use that it is recommended by plastic surgeons and dermatologists throughout the world. Talc and paraben free, non-comedogenic and with virtually no allergy risk, the products are suitable for the most sensitive skins, and their avoidance of harsh and toxic chemicals means they are particularly recommended during pregnancy. They also offer broad-spectrum UVB and UVA protection. For more information visit www.janeiredaleuk.eu or phone Landmark Distributors Ltd on 0208 450 7111.

ORGANIC CLOTHING

Chemical-free clothing is kinder to your baby's sensitive skin. Organics for Kids make beautiful clothes for babies and young children, in their British factory, using a range of fairly traded, organic textiles. Visit www.organicsforkids.co.uk

ORGANIC, VOC-FREE PAINT

Ecos water-based organic paint is free of all pesticides, herbicides and toxins, and is odourless and VOC- and solvent-free. Conventional gloss and emulsion paints contain solvents that release low-level toxic emissions in the form of volatile organic compounds (VOCs) for years. This is of particular concern when used in babies' nurseries, but the Ecos range offers a safe alternative. See www.ecosorganicpaints.com

PREGNANCY AND BREAST-FEEDING SUPPORT PILLOWS

The Dream Genii™ pillow supports your body to aid restful sleep during pregnancy and helps you to sleep on your left side to encourage your baby into the optimum position for birth. Dream Genii™ can also be used as a feeding pillow. Visit www.dreamgenii.com

My Brest Friend is the most supportive pillow for successful breast-feeding, with a wrap-around design, back rest and firm cushion to support you and your baby, making it the choice of a number of health professionals. Visit www.mybrestfriend.com or www.expressyourselfmums.co.uk

PURFLO COT MATTRESSES AND BEDDING

The revolutionary PurFlo® mattress is the world's only completely washable mattress and the most hygienic sleeping environment for your baby. The unique, fully breathable SleepSurface™ fits over a hollow frame and comfortably supports your baby or child better than any conventional mattress while the protective outer valance features Allergy UK-approved Amicor™ pure – an intelligent fibre that dispels household dust mites, bacteria, fungi and even repels the growth of MRSA. Visit www.purflo.com for more information.

TEETHING NECKLACES

Hazelwood appears to neutralise acidity in the body, helping with all sorts of medical complaints including teething pain. These baby-safe necklaces are used by parents worldwide as a natural alternative to drugs to help relieve the discomfort of teething. Visit www.tearlessteething.com for more information.

TENS MACHINES FOR NATURAL PAIN RELIEF DURING LABOUR

TENS has a reputation as one of the safest, most effective forms of pain control during childbirth. Widely approved by medical professionals, this natural treatment encourages the release of the body's own pain-relieving hormones and stimulates nerves to block pain signals. MamaTENS offer portable units for sale or for hire to enable women to actively manage their own pain relief, to encourage a mobile, drug-free labour with no side effects. For more information visit www.mama-tens.info or phone 0845 230 4647.

SWADDLING

Swaddling has been shown to help encourage sleep and soothe fractious babies. The Puckababy is a swaddling sleeping bag for the first six months, cocooning the baby to make them feel secure while still leaving room for healthy physical development. The Puckabag is a follow-on sleeping bag to further encourage older babies into good sleeping habits. For more information or to order visit www.puckababy.com

You can also buy traditional swaddling blankets to wrap your baby securely to soothe them and aid sleep; Swaddle Designs sell a range of beautiful organic swaddling blankets; visit www.swaddledesigns.com

Foods

CACAO (RAW CHOCOLATE POWDER) AND OTHER 'SUPERFOODS'

Detox Your World imports raw, organic superfoods such as cacao (raw chocolate powder) for wholesale across Europe. You can find the Detox Your World range in good whole food shops and online at www.detoxyourworld.com

CHERRYACTIVE

CherryActive is an antioxidant-rich concentrate made from 100 per cent Montmorency cherries. With no added sugars, preservatives or other additives, CherryActive Concentrate dilutes into a great-tasting, low-GL cherry juice that counts towards yours and your family's five-a-day target. It is available from www.cherryactive.co.uk and from your local health shop.

LOW-GL RICE

Maharani low-GL rice is a white rice with the health benefits of brown rice. It is available from Totally Nourish. Visit totallynourish.com.

ORGANIC FOODS

For details of organic fruit/veg box scheme providers in your area, visit the Soil Association website at www.soilassociation.org or phone 0117 314 5000.

TURNHAM GREEN HEALTHY HAMPERS

Turnham Green is a gourmet gift company providing delicious pantry products with a nutritional and ethical twist. Each product is carefully sourced using a combination of organic, local and fair trade ingredients. They deliver the very next day anywhere in the UK. For more information visit www.turnham-green.co.uk or phone 0797 221 6993.

VIRGIN COCONUT OIL

For superb-quality, fairly traded, certified organic virgin coconut oil (retail/wholesale) contact Coconut Connections Ltd, 5 Sycamore Dene, Chesham, Bucks HP5 3JT. Phone 01494 771419 or order from their website www.virgincoconutoil.co.uk

XYLITOL

Xylitol is a natural alternative to sugar and artificial sweeteners, with a very low GI value of seven; 10 times lower than sugar, with several other health benefits as well. Perfect Sweet xylitol is available in selected Sainsbury's, Holland & Barrett, Waitrose and independent stockists. For more details, visit www.perfectsweet.co.uk. Xylitol is also available from Totally Nourish (see below).

Supplements

For pregnancy multivitamins, antioxidants, homocysteine-lowering formulas, essential fats and probiotics, the following companies produce good-quality supplements that are widely available in the UK:
BioCare Available in most health food shops. Tel: 0121 433 3727. Website: www.biocare.co.uk
Nordic Naturals sell high quality fish oils. Website: www.nordicnaturals.com
Solgar Available in most health food shops. Contact Solgar on 01442 890355 for your nearest supplier. Website: www.solgar.co.uk
Totally Nourish offers a wide range of health products, from supplements to water filters, including xylitol and CherryActive, by mail and

online. But you can also order by freephone on 0800 085 7749, or visit www.totallynourish.com

And in other regions

South Africa Bioharmony produce a wide range of products in South Africa and other African countries. For details of your nearest supplier contact 0860 888 339 or visit www.bioharmony.co.za
Australia Solgar supplements are available in Australia. Contact Solgar on 1800 029 871 (free call) for your nearest supplier. Website: www.solgar.com.au. Another good brand is Blackmores.
New Zealand Biocare products are available in New Zealand. Contact Aurora Natural Therapies, 4 La Trobe Track, KareKare, Waitakere City, Auckland 1232, New Zealand. www.Aurora.org.nz
Singapore Biocare and Solgar products are available in Singapore. Please contact Essential Living on 6276 1380 for your nearest supplier or visit www.essliv.com

Useful Books

FERTILITY MONITORING AND NATURAL FAMILY PLANNING
The Manual of Natural Family Planning by Anna Flynn and Melissa Brooks (Thorsons/HarperCollins). Also visit the website www.fertilityfriend.com

WEANING
Baby-led Weaning – helping your baby to love good food, by Gill Rapley and Tracey Murkett, 2008, Vermilion

INDEX